98 avoid bad

go to bed [illegible]

don't gamble

or hang out

in pool halls

(Chapter 31)

love mother (90)

work hard 95, 144

self reliant 85

honesty 100

Do your duty (60)

money 64

education 93

men & women 54

reliability 82

14

rags to riches

respect elders

60

64

98

75

86

Horatio Alger Jr.

HORATIO ALGER, JR.

STRUGGLING UPWARD

or, Luke Larkin's Luck

With a New Introduction by

RALPH D. GARDNER

Author of *Horatio Alger; or, The American Hero Era*

Dover Publications, Inc.
New York

Published in Canada by General Publishing Company, Ltd., 30 Lesmill Road, Don Mills, Toronto, Ontario.
Published in the United Kingdom by Constable and Company, Ltd.

This Dover edition, first published in 1984, is an unabridged republication of the work originally published serially in *The Golden Argosy*, March 13–June 19, 1886 (first book publication: Porter & Coates, Philadelphia, 1890). A new introduction has been specially prepared for this edition by Ralph D. Gardner.

Manufactured in the United States of America
Dover Publications, Inc., 31 East 2nd Street, Mineola, N.Y. 11501

Library of Congress Cataloging in Publication Data

Alger, Horatio, 1832–1899.
Struggling upward, or, Luke Larkin's luck.

Reprint. Originally published: Philadelphia : Porter & Coates, 1890.
Summary: Relates the adventures of Luke Larkin, a poor boy of the nineteenth century, who perseveres against many odds and gains success.
I. Title. II. Title: Struggling upward. III. Title: Luke Larkin's luck.
PZ7.A395St 1984 [Fic] 84-7977
ISBN 0-486-24737-6 (pbk.)

THE RETURN OF HORATIO ALGER!

by

Ralph D. Gardner

In 1982 a postage stamp was issued to celebrate the sesquicentennial of Horatio Alger's birth.[1] This event attracted far more attention than the average commemorative-stamp issue, with official observations in a dozen cities, extensive news and feature coverage by print and broadcast media, and a Public Broadcasting Service television special.[2]

For many Americans, this was their introduction to the author who wrote action-packed thrillers about sturdy, self-reliant lads who struggled upward against enormous odds. After a half-century of unrivaled appeal, their popularity having crested during the years of World War I, Alger's books were replaced by others featuring a new generation of heroes who sped across the continent on motorcycles and piloted aircraft above the clouds to foreign lands.

Horatio Alger's *name*, however, has remained a permanent part of our language. It has become a colloquialism that invariably describes a spectacular rise to fame and fortune. Like few other names, it sparks immediate recognition.

Acknowledging this, *The New York Times* called Alger "the most successful writer of boys' stories in the whole of American literature," adding: "his heroes always seemed to succeed through a combination of 'luck and pluck.'"[3]

Little surprise, then, was the inevitable return of Alger's books. Parents and grandparents sought them—often at hefty auction prices or from antiquarian booksellers—to offer their children and grandchildren wholesome, exciting alternatives to currently available reading and other entertainment. Often these old-timers, themselves nostalgia-smitten and delighted by this renewed acquaintance with almost forgotten pleasures, searched for additional Alger titles.

Just as significant, and long overdue, is the appreciation of Alger's writings in universities, where they are studied for their unique, pivotal place in American juvenile literature. Within that literature, Alger's stories can be clearly seen to separate earlier, heavily moralized, didactic tales from later arrivals that trade heavily upon spectacular inventions of the industrialized twentieth century.

It is, therefore, surprising how few can recall exactly who Horatio Alger was. I've heard him identified variously—and incorrectly—as a poor, honest boy who worked hard and got very rich; as the hero of a long series of success stories, who always married the boss's daughter; and even as a pen name of Charles Dickens.

Let me assure you that Horatio Alger was the real name of a real person.[4] He wrote 110 books; more, if you add a couple of slender volumes of poetry. He also made occasional attempts at adult novels that exasperated his publishers. Fearing that these could damage Alger's enormous popularity among young readers, they insisted that the books be issued anonymously or under pseudonyms.[5]

It is a fact that, from Civil War days until well past the turn of the century, most boys and many girls who were brought up in the United States were delighted with Alger's characters and plots. They read, reread, swapped, and borrowed books with such alliterative titles as *Slow and Sure, Try and Trust*, and *Strong and Steady*. Public libraries had shelves filled with them. They were awarded as school prizes, ministers recommended them from pulpits, and, unlike blood-and-thunder dime novels—with lurid descriptions of frontier violence—Alger's stories could be read in the parlor.

Although he had been a sickly child, and was all his life affected by asthma, Alger became a Phi Beta Kappa graduate of Harvard,[6] a teacher, newspaper editor in Boston, and, for a brief period, a minister on Cape Cod.[7] As a classics student of Henry Wadsworth Longfellow, Alger became his professor's disciple, and actually planned to become a poet. Although he turned out dozens of sentimental verses that appeared in periodicals,[8] he soon discovered the more lucrative market for adult fiction.[9] When, upon moving to New York in 1866, he observed the pitiful plight of the city's abandoned street children who worked as bootblacks and newsboys, he wrote *Ragged Dick*. It created a sensation, became Alger's first best-seller, and set the pattern for virtually every other book he wrote.[10]

Following the extraordinary success of *Ragged Dick* and other rags-to-riches novels that quickly followed, Alger's publisher, A. K. Loring, lauded him as "the dominating figure of our new era. In his books he has captured the spirit of reborn America. The turmoil of the streets is in them. You can hear the rattle of pails on the farms. Above all, you can hear the cry of triumph of the oppressed over the oppressor. What Alger has done is to portray the soul—the ambitious soul—of the country!"

What was Alger's captivating formula? Let me give you the typical Alger tale in capsule form:

As most stories begin, our hero is about fifteen years old, the son of a widowed mother or an orphan of vaguely mysterious background. Whether a country lad or city urchin, after a few pages he finds himself adrift on the cobbled streets of lower Broadway with only a few cents in his pocket. But he is ambitious and eagerly accepts menial work. From the beginning he has enemies: street-corner bullies, a brutal guardian, swaggering snobs, and a host of other evildoers.

He soon performs a heroic deed, pulling a child from the path of a runaway horse, rescuing someone from being sandbagged and robbed, diving into the East River to save a life, or flagging down a speeding train. He also returns lots of wallets and lost jewelry.

In appreciation, he is rewarded with a better job, usually as a clerk. At this point he is introduced to his benefactor's winsome, flirtatious daughter, who finds him fascinating.

Because he displays initiative and shrewdness, our hero is sent upon a hazardous journey. This involves his courage and detective skills. He faces a variety of dangers, during the course of which he accidentally meets a person who helps him uncover the mystery of his own past. The mission is always a triumph, and he achieves moderate success and middle-class respectability before he is eighteen. There is the inevitable happy ending, often with the mortgaged homestead saved from the clutches of a scheming village squire, and enemies scattered in disarray.

Alger's stories definitely are robust, and he was inventive enough to inject a bit of the devil into his heroes. Some smoke penny cigars, guzzle whiskey at three cents a shot, and—when they have cash to spare—attend the disreputable Bowery Theatre. One is known as The Bully of the Village,[11] and another enters the narrative burglarizing the town house of a wealthy gentleman who, at the story's conclusion, turns out to be his grandfather.[12]

Of course, these character flaws are quickly overcome. The boys study in the evenings, determined to better themselves. The attraction of Alger's stories to many readers was that they sparked the readers' own resolve that "If Ragged Dick can do it, so can I!"

And if you'll accept the word of more than 300 men and women who once read Alger and agree that he inspired them to struggle upward from humble beginnings to high positions, you may discover—as they did—that his novels contain an added bonus: *a blueprint for success*. Such noted leaders include Presidents Eisenhower and Reagan, Ralph J. Bunche, Conrad Hilton, Arthur J. Goldberg, Lowell Thomas, Clare Boothe Luce, Gene Autry, Thurgood Marshall, Pearl S. Buck, Eddie Rickenbacker, and many, many more. All of these award recipients of the Horatio Alger Association of Distinguished Americans have recognized and applied the Horatio Alger blueprint.[13]

During the years since World War II, Alger's works have become an increasingly fertile field for analysis, and some analysts have read into these uncomplicated tales psychological undercurrents that would have astonished Alger. His sole purpose, I am convinced, was to provide crackling good, fast-paced entertainment. On the other hand, the comments of modern day carpers—who apply late-twentieth-century standards to these nineteenth-century relics (which is like comparing supersonic aircraft to covered wagons)—reckon without the verdict of youngsters who have read these books in relatively recent decades.

In 1961—as on other occasions—I gave modest collections of Algers to Children's Aid Society libraries,[14] asking the librarian to let me know some reactions of those who examined these displays. I learned that almost all who scanned a page or two took the book home to read. Upon returning it, they enthusiastically asked for other Alger titles.

One of the most popular among those tattered treasures was *Struggling Upward*, the story you are about to read. You are going to enjoy this adventure of Luke Larkin, "the son of a carpenter's widow. . . . He had a pleasant expression, and a bright, resolute look, a warm heart, and a clear intellect, and was probably, in spite of his poverty, the most popular boy in Groveton. . . . He filled the position of janitor at the school which he attended, sweeping out twice a week and making the fires." For this he received a dollar a week. He also "worked where he could, helping farmers in hay-time, and ready to do odd jobs for any one."

After a number of episodes in Groveton, situated thirty-five miles from New York, Luke journeys by railroad—a trip that "was a trifle over an hour"—to the metropolis. We join him on a confidential investigation that takes him to Chicago, onward to Minnesota, and beyond, to a mining camp in the Black Hills of the Dakota Territory. En route, he faces the perils of a larcenous con-man and a pair of highway bandits before bringing his search to an exciting conclusion at a shack in Fenton's Gulch, a day's ride from Deadwood.

Like most Alger novels, *Struggling Upward* first appeared as a serial. During the period when Alger dominated the hero-fiction field, publication in weekly or monthly story-papers most often represented an author's major source of income. For works that were later issued as books, writers generally received a flat fee. Alger was a cagey enough businessman to command top serial fees and, contrary to standard practice, hardcover advances and the highest royalties. From at least one of his many publishers—Porter & Coates—he received shares in their corporation.

The first installment of *Struggling Upward* was featured in Frank

Munsey's *The Golden Argosy* on March 13, 1886; the story concluded in the issue dated June 19.

Munsey, a former Maine farm boy proud of his own rise to eminence as a New York publisher, regularly featured success fiction, personality sketches of people who had struggled upward, and editorials urging readers to strive toward their own goals.

Assuring the public that "The Golden Argosy—freighted with treasures for boys and girls—is a safe paper for the family, filled with stories and other matter of the highest character," he offered, besides Alger, works by the contemporary favorites Annie Ashmore, Edward S. Ellis, and Frank Converse, among others.

Luke Larkin's tale opens with a dramatic race to win a Waterbury pocket watch. The possession of such a timepiece apparently was the ambition of many boys of that era, for Munsey gave them as prizes to those who signed up new subscribers. He also offered an $8.00 Waterbury "nickel silver stem-winder with handsome chain and charm" for $1.50 to all who sent in only their own subscription. Advertisements showed glistening Waterbury watches, including the $3.50 model, which "is carried today by bankers, merchants, scientific men, clerks and messengers, army and navy men, traders, conductors and engineers."

Other frequently advertised products were bicycles, ice skates, foreign postage stamps, a one-mile signal whistle for 25 cents ("valuable on the farm"), chromos, and pianos, as well as instruction in telegraphy, penmanship, and sewing.

Patent-medicine ads listed Dr. Kline's Great Nerve Restorer ("all fits stopped"); Adamson's Botanic Cough Balsam ("for the cure of croup, asthma and whooping cough"); Wilcox's Anti-Corpulence Pills ("positively reduce superfluous flesh"); a cure for "drunkenness or the liquor habit"; Bruceline's Hair Tonic ("restores gray hair and beard to its original color . . . causes hair to grow on bald heads"); and Mellin's Food for infants and invalids ("the only perfect substitute for mother's milk").

Business opportunities were advertised by the Empire Knitting Company ("ladies to do worsted caps at home. Steady work. Good pay"); Dr. Scott's Electric Corsets ("1000 agents wanted at once. Only respectable persons wanted"); and McAllister Opticians' Magic Lanterns and Stereopticons ("a profitable business for the man with small capital").

Weekly features included puzzles, contests, jokes and conundrums, a swapping column, and readers' inquiries that elicited such replies as "large noses indicate strong character . . . a typewriter was made and used in 1867 . . . the eagle cent of 1858 is worth only its face value . . .

the New York-New Jersey Tunnel has been stopped until more money can be gotten."

Editorially, Munsey expressed opinions in favor of industriousness, good manners, fine penmanship, and care of animals, and against smoking, drinking, and laziness. He frequently commented upon current topics: "The art of ballooning has received a great deal of attention lately, and may be used in many and unthought of ways in the future." "A wholesale destruction of small birds is carried on in the interest of ladies' bonnets." "Wealthy New Yorkers whose homes are near the Central Park menagerie have been petitioning for its removal as a nuisance. They say the lions and wolves roar and howl at night." One often-repeated editorial reiterated his own philosophy: "Poor boys can rise. No boy need despair because he is poor. Most of the great men in America rose to eminence from poverty. So many have done so that we cannot enumerate them all. Poverty is no bar to success."

Struggling Upward, one of more than forty Alger adventures serialized by Munsey, remained a favorite throughout and after the author's long reign. After initial book publication by Porter & Coates, in 1890—during which year eight Alger stories were issued as books, and another half-dozen were serialized—no fewer than twenty-one publishers reprinted this popular title. It was released in England[15] and later in a Japanese translation titled *Secret Small Box*.[16] It has also been rewritten as a three-act play.

Struggling Upward is, indeed, a rediscovered classic. It ranks high—along with *Ragged Dick, Tom the Bootblack*, and *Phil the Fiddler*—on collectors' lists of Alger favorites.

Now slip back in time. A hundred years or so. Get lost for a few hours in that long-ago era when the air was sweeter, the pace more relaxed, and the skyline lower. If you've read Horatio Alger before, you probably can't wait to get there. If *Struggling Upward* is your introduction to his delight-filled world, you're off to a fine start. However, this word of caution: savoring its magic can give you a hearty appetite for more!

NOTES

1. Alger was born at Chelsea—now Revere—Massachusetts, on January 13, 1832. When the 20-cent stamp was finally approved for issue after having been twice rejected, the nation's press hailed it as "a typical Horatio Alger success story," noting that the members of the Horatio Alger Society's Sesquicentennial Stamp Committee had personally lobbied the Citizens' Stamp Advisory Panel and every member of Congress in order to enlist their support. On April 30, 1982, Postmaster General William F. Bolger participated in the main ceremony at Willow Grove, Pennsylvania, site of the Alger Society's annual convention. During the weeks that followed, observances were held at Natick, Massachusetts—where Alger died, in 1899—and other cities.

2. Titled *American Dreamers*, the television documentary was produced in cooperation with the Horatio Alger Association of Distinguished Americans. Initial airing was September 14, 1982.

3. Samuel Tower, "United States Lists Its 1982 Commemoratives," *The New York Times*, 24 January 1982.

4. Alger invariably signed his name as Horatio Alger, Jr., even after the death of his father, a prominent Unitarian minister and Massachusetts legislator.

5. Ralph D. Gardner, *Horatio Alger; or, The American Hero Era* (Mendota, Illinois: Wayside Press, 1964; reissued, New York: Arco, 1978). See "The Bibliography of Alger's Works," starting on p. 394, Wayside edition; p. 388, Arco edition. Alger pen names include Arthur Hamilton, Arthur Lee Putnam, Julian Starr, etc.; see pp. 369–72, Wayside edition; pp. 366–68, Arco edition.

6. Alger was a member of the Harvard Class of 1852, graduating eighth in a class of 88. See Grace Williamson Edes, *Annals of the Harvard Class of 1852* (Cambridge, Massachusetts: Harvard University Press, 1922), pp. 54, 121, 193, *et passim*.

7. Ralph D. Gardner, "Foreword," *A Fancy of Hers / The Disagreeable Woman*, by Horatio Alger, Jr. (New York: Van Nostrand Reinhold Com-

pany, 1981), pp. 7–15. Alger was engaged as minister of the First Parish Unitarian Church, at Brewster, Massachusetts, in November 1864. He resigned in March 1866, after having been accused by a church-appointed committee of involvement in a homosexual incident.

8. Gardner, *Horatio Alger*. . . . See list, pp. 486–91, Wayside edition; pp. 481–86, Arco edition. The exact number of Alger's poems is unknown, as they often appeared anonymously and in long-forgotten publications.

9. Gardner, "Foreword," *A Fancy of Hers* . . ., pp. 16–19. The 1981 edition marks the first publication of these two novels in book form under Alger's byline. A slightly different version of *A Fancy of Hers* was published anonymously as *The New Schoolma'am* (Boston: A. K. Loring, 1877). *The Disagreeable Woman* (New York: G. W. Dillingham, 1895) was issued under the Alger pen name Julian Starr. Other adult novels—all appearing in the New York *Sun* between 1857 and 1860—include: *Hugo the Deformed, Madeleine the Temptress, The Secret Drawer, The Cooper's Ward, The Mad Heiress*, and *The Discarded Son*.

10. *Ragged Dick; or, Street Life in New York* (Boston: A. K. Loring, 1868). Alger's eighth book, it was serialized in *Student and Schoolmate*, January through December 1867.

11. *Tom Temple's Career* (New York: A. L. Burt, 1888).

12. *Adrift in New York; or, Tom and Florence Braving the World* (New York: A. L. Burt, 1904).

13. *Only in America; Opportunity Still Knocks*, Volume II (New York: Horatio Alger Association of Distinguished Americans, 1982), pp. 199–207.

14. The event was reported in *The New York Times* for January 13, 1961, and in several other newspapers.

15. Published as a paperback in the Garfield Library (London: Aldine, 1891).

16. (Tokyo: Kodansha, [1971?]).

17. By Rilla Carlisle, pen name of Anne Coulter Martens (Chicago: Dramatic, 1946).

STRUGGLING UPWARD

or, Luke Larkin's Luck

CHAPTER I

THE WATERBURY WATCH

ONE Saturday afternoon in January a lively and animated group of boys were gathered on the western side of a large pond in the village of Groveton. Prominent among them was a tall, pleasant-looking young man of twenty-two, the teacher of the Center Grammar School, Frederic Hooper, A.B., a recent graduate of Yale College. Evidently there was something of importance on foot. What it was may be learned from the words of the teacher.

"Now, boys," he said, holding in his hand a Waterbury watch, of neat pattern, "I offer this watch as a prize to the boy who will skate across the pond and back in the least time. You will all start together, at a given signal, and make your way to the mark which I have placed at the western end of the lake, skate around it, and return to this point. Do you fully understand?"

"Yes, sir!" exclaimed the boys, unanimously.

Before proceeding, it may be well to refer more particularly to some of the boys who were to engage in the contest.

First, in his own estimation, came Randolph Duncan, son of Prince Duncan, president of the Groveton Bank, and a prominent town official. Prince Duncan was supposed to be a rich man, and lived in a style quite beyond that of his neighbors. Randolph was his only son, a boy of sixteen, and felt that in social position and blue blood he was without a peer in the village. He was a tall, athletic boy, and disposed to act the part of boss among the Groveton boys.

Next came a boy similar in age and physical strength, but in other respects very different from the young aristocrat. This was Luke Larkin, the son of a carpenter's widow, living on narrow means, and so compelled to exercise the strictest economy. Luke worked where he could, helping the farmers in hay-time, and ready to do odd jobs for any one in the village who desired his services. He filled the position of janitor at the school which he attended, sweeping out twice a week and making the fires. He had a pleasant expression, and a bright, resolute look, a warm heart, and a clear intellect, and was probably, in spite of his poverty, the most popular boy in Groveton. In this respect he was the opposite of Randolph Duncan, whose assumption of superiority and desire to "boss" the other boys prevented him from having any real friends. He had two or three companions, who flattered him and submitted to his caprices because they thought it looked well to be on good terms with the young aristocrat.

These two boys were looked upon as the chief contestants for the prize offered by their teacher. Opinions differed as to which would win.

"I think Luke will get the watch," said Fred Acken, a younger boy.

"I don't know about that," said Tom Harper. "Randolph skates just as well, and he has a pair of club skates. His father sent to New York for them last week. They're beauties, I tell you. Randolph says they cost ten dollars."

"Of course that gives him the advantage," said Percy Hall. "Look at Luke's old-fashioned wooden skates! They would be dear at fifty cents!"

"It's a pity Luke hasn't a better pair," said Harry Wright. "I don't think the contest is a fair one. Luke ought to have an allowance of twenty rods, to make up for the difference in skates."

"He wouldn't accept it," said Linton Tomkins, the son of a manufacturer in Groveton, who was an intimate friend of Luke, and preferred to associate with him, though Randolph had made advances toward intimacy, Linton being the only boy in the village whom he regarded as his social equal. "I offered him my club skates, but he said he would take the chances with his own."

Linton was the only boy who had a pair of skates equal to Randolph's. He, too, was a contestant, but, being three years younger than Luke and Randolph, had no expectation of rivaling them.

Randolph had his friends near him, administering the adulation he so much enjoyed.

"I have no doubt you'll get the watch, Randolph," said Sam Noble. "You're a better skater any day than Luke Larkin."

"Of course you are!" chimed in Tom Harper.

"The young janitor doesn't think so," said Randolph, his lips curling.

"Oh, he's conceited enough to think he can beat you, I make no doubt," said Sam.

"On those old skates, too! They look as if Adam might have used them when he was a boy!"

This sally of Tom's created a laugh.

"His skates are old ones, to be sure," said Randolph, who was quick-sighted enough to understand that any remark of this kind might dim the luster of his expected victory. "His skates are old enough, but they are just as good for skating as mine."

"They won't win him the watch, though," said Sam.

"I don't care for the watch myself," said Randolph, loftily. "I've got a silver one now, and am to have a gold one when I'm eighteen. But I want to show that I am the best skater. Besides, father has promised me ten dollars if I win."

"I wish I had ten dollars," said Sam, enviously.

He was the son of the storekeeper, and his father allowed him only ten cents a week pocket-money, so that ten dollars in his eyes was a colossal fortune.

"I have no doubt you would, Sam," said Tom, joyously; "but you couldn't be trusted with so much money. You'd go down to New York and try to buy out A. T. Stewart."

"Are you ready, boys?" asked Mr. Hooper.

Most of the boys responded promptly in the affirmative; but Luke, who had been tightening his straps, said quickly: "I am not ready, Mr. Hooper. My strap has broken!"

"Indeed, Luke, I am sorry to hear it," said the teacher, approaching and examining the fracture. "As matters stand, you can't skate."

Randolph's eyes brightened. Confident as he professed to feel, he knew that his chances of success would be greatly increased by Luke's withdrawal from the list.

"The prize is yours now," whispered Tom.

"It was before," answered Randolph, conceitedly.

Poor Luke looked disappointed. He knew that he had at least an even chance of winning, and he wanted the watch. Several of his friends of his own age had watches, either silver or Waterbury, and this seemed, in his circumstances, the only chance of securing one. Now he was apparently barred out.

"It's a pity you shouldn't skate, Luke," said Mr. Hooper, in a tone of sympathy. "You are one of the best skaters, and had an excellent chance of winning the prize. Is there any boy willing to lend Luke his skates?"

"I will," said Frank Acken.

"My dear boy," said the teacher, "you forget that your feet are several sizes smaller than Luke's."

"I didn't think of that," replied Frank, who was only twelve years old.

"You may use my skates, Luke," said Linton Tomkins. "I think they will fit you."

Linton was only thirteen, but he was unusually large for his age.

"You are very kind, Linton," said Luke, "but that will keep you out of the race."

"I stand no chance of winning," said Linton, "and I will do my skating afterward."

"I don't think that fair," said Randolph, with a frown. "Each boy ought to use his own skates."

"There is nothing unfair about it," said the teacher, "except that Luke is placed at disadvantage in using a pair of skates he is unaccustomed to."

Randolph did not dare gainsay the teacher, but he looked sullen.

"Mr. Hooper is always favoring that beggar!" he said in a low voice, to Tom Harper.

"Of course he is!" chimed in the toady.

"You are very kind, Linny," said Luke, regarding his friend affectionately. "I won't soon forget it."

"Oh, it's all right, Luke," said Linton. "Now go in and win!"

CHAPTER II

TOM HARPER'S ACCIDENT

TOM HARPER and Sam Noble were not wholly disinterested in their championship of Randolph. They were very ordinary skaters, and stood no chance of winning the match themselves. They wished Randolph to win, for each hoped, as he had a silver watch himself already, he might give the Waterbury to his faithful friend and follower. Nothing in Randolph's character warranted such a hope, for he was by no means generous or openhanded, but each thought that he might open his heart on this occasion. Indeed, Tom ventured to hint as much.

"I suppose, Randolph," he said, "if you win the watch you will give it to me?"

"Why should I?" asked Randolph, surveying Tom with a cold glance.

"You've got a nice silver watch yourself, you know."

"I might like to have two watches."

"You'll have the ten dollars your father promised you."

"What if I have? What claim have you on me?"

Tom drew near and whispered something in Randolph's ear.

"I'll see about it," said Randolph, nodding.

"Are you ready?" asked the teacher, once more.

"Aye, aye!" responded the boys.

"One—two—three—go!"

The boys darted off like arrows from a bow. Luke made a late start, but before they were half across the pond he was even with Randolph, and both were leading. Randolph looked sidewise, and shut his mouth tight as he saw his hated rival on equal terms with him and threatening to pass him. It would be humiliating in the extreme, he thought, to be beaten by such a boy.

But beaten he seemed likely to be, for Luke was soon a rod in advance and slowly gaining. Slowly, for Randolph was really a fine skater and had no rival except Luke. But Luke was his superior, as seemed likely to be proved.

Though only these two stood any chance of final success, all the boys kept up the contest.

A branch of a tree had been placed at the western end of the pond, and this was the mark around which the boys were to skate. Luke made the circuit first, Randolph being about half a dozen rods behind. After him came the rest of the boys in procession, with one exception. This exception was Tom Harper, who apparently gave up the contest when half-way across, and began skating about, here and there, apparently waiting for his companions to return.

"Tom Harper has given up his chance," said Linton to the teacher.

"So it seems," replied Mr. Hooper, "but he probably had no expectation of succeeding."

"I should think he would have kept on with the rest. I would have done so, though my chance would have been no better than his."

Indeed, it seemed strange that Tom should have given up

so quickly. It soon appeared that it was not caprice, but that he had an object in view, and that a very discreditable one.

He waited till the boys were on their way back. By this time Luke was some eight rods in advance of his leading competitor. Then Tom began to be on the alert. As Luke came swinging on to victory he suddenly placed himself in his way. Luke's speed was so great that he could not check himself. He came into collision with Tom, and in an instant both were prostrate. Tom, however, got the worst of it. He was thrown violently backward, falling on the back of his head, and lay stunned and motionless on the ice. Luke fell over him, but was scarcely hurt at all. He was up again in an instant, and might still have kept the lead, but instead he got down on his knees beside Tom and asked anxiously: "Are you much hurt, Tom?"

Tom didn't immediately answer, but lay breathing heavily, with his eyes still closed.

Meanwhile, Randolph, with a smile of triumph, swept on to his now assured victory. Most of the boys, however, stopped and gathered round Luke and Tom.

This accident had been watched with interest and surprise from the starting-point.

"Tom must be a good deal hurt," said Linton. "What could possibly have made him get in Luke's way?"

"I don't know," said the teacher, slowly; "it looks strange."

"It almost seemed as if he got in the way on purpose," Linton continued.

"He is a friend of Randolph Duncan, is he not?" asked the teacher, abruptly.

"They are together about all the time."

"Ha!" commented the teacher, as if struck by an idea. He didn't, however, give expression to the thought in his mind.

A minute more, and Randolph swept into the presence of the teacher.

"I believe I have won?" he said, with a smile of gratification on his countenance.

"You have come in first," said the teacher coldly.

"Luke was considerably ahead when he ran into Tom," suggested Linton.

"That's not my lookout," said Randolph, shrugging his shoulders. "The point is that I have come in first."

"Tom Harper is a friend of yours, is he not?" asked the teacher.

"Oh, yes!" answered Randolph, indifferently.

"He seems to be a good deal hurt. It was very strange that he got in Luke's way."

"So it was," said Randolph, without betraying much interest.

"Will you lend me your skates, Randolph?" asked Linton. "I should like to go out and see if I can help Tom in any way."

If any other boy than Linton had made the request, Randolph would have declined, but he wished, if possible, to add Linton to his list of friends, and graciously consented.

Before Linton could reach the spot, Tom had been assisted to his feet, and, with a dazed expression, assisted on either side by Luke and Edmund Blake, was on his way back to the starting-point.

"What made you get in my way, Tom?" asked Luke, puzzled.

"I don't know," answered Tom, sullenly.

"Are you much hurt?"

"I think my skull must be fractured," moaned Tom.

"Oh, not so bad as that," said Luke, cheerfully. "I've fallen on my head myself, but I got over it."

"You didn't fall as hard as I did," groaned Tom.

"No, I presume not; but heads are hard, and I guess you'll be all right in a few days."

Tom had certainly been severely hurt. There was a swelling on the back of his head almost as large as a hen's egg.

"You've lost the watch, Luke," said Frank Acken. "Randolph has got in first."

"Yes, I supposed he would," answered Luke, quietly.

"And there is Linton Tomkins coming to meet us on Randolph's skates."

"Randolph is sitting down on a log taking it easy. What is your loss, Luke, is his gain."

"Yes."

"I think he might have come back to inquire after you, Tom, as you are a friend of his."

Tom looked resentfully at Randolph, and marked his complacent look, and it occurred to him also that the friend he had risked so much to serve was very ungrateful. But he hoped now, at any rate, to get the watch, and thought it prudent to say nothing.

The boys had now reached the shore.

"Hope you're not much hurt, Tom?" said Randolph, in a tone of mild interest.

"I don't know but my skull is fractured," responded Tom, bitterly.

"Oh, I guess not. It's the fortune of war. Well, I got in first."

Randolph waited for congratulations, but none came. All the boys looked serious, and more than one suspected that there had been foul play. They waited for the teacher to speak.

CHAPTER III

RANDOLPH GETS THE WATCH

"IT IS true," said the teacher, slowly. "Randolph has won the race."

Randolph's face lighted up with exultation.

"But it is also evident," continued Mr. Hooper, "that he would not have succeeded but for the unfortunate collision between Luke Larkin and Tom Harper."

Here some of Luke's friends brightened up.

"I don't know about that," said Randolph. "At any rate, I came in first."

"I watched the race closely," said the teacher, "and I have no doubt on the subject. Luke had so great a lead that he would surely have won the race."

"But he didn't," persisted Randolph, doggedly

"He did not, as we all know. It is also clear that had he not stopped to ascertain the extent of Tom's injuries he still might have won."

"That's so!" said half a dozen boys.

"Therefore I cannot accept the result as indicating the superiority of the successful contestant."

"I think I am entitled to the prize," said Randolph.

"I concede that; but, under the circumstances, I suggest to you that it would be graceful and proper to waive your claim and try the race over again."

The boys applauded, with one or two exceptions.

"I won't consent to that, Mr. Hooper," said Randolph, frowning. "I've won the prize fairly and I want it."

"I am quite willing Randolph should have it, sir," said Luke. "I think I should have won it if I had not stopped with Tom, but that doesn't affect the matter one way or the other. Randolph came in first, as he says, and I think he is entitled to the watch."

"Then," said Mr. Hooper, gravely, "there is nothing more to be said. Randolph, come forward and receive the prize."

Randolph obeyed with alacrity, and received the Waterbury watch from the hands of Mr. Hooper. The boys stood in silence and offered no congratulations.

"Now, let me say," said the teacher, "that I cannot understand why there was any collision at all. Tom Harper, why did you get in Luke's way?"

"Because I was a fool, sir," answered Tom, smarting from his injuries, and the evident indifference of Randolph, in whose cause he had incurred them.

"That doesn't answer my question. Why did you act like a fool, as you expressed it?"

"I thought I could get out of the way in time," stammered Tom, who did not dare to tell the truth.

"You had no other reason?" asked the teacher, searchingly.

"No, sir. What other reason could I have?" said Tom, but his manner betrayed confusion.

"Indeed, I don't know," returned the teacher, quietly. "Your action, however, spoiled Luke's chances and insured the success of Randolph."

"And got me a broken head," muttered Tom, placing his hand upon the swelling at the back of his head.

"Yes, you got the worst of it. I advise you to go home and apply cold water or any other remedy your mother may suggest."

Randolph had already turned away, meaning to return home. Tom joined him. Randolph would gladly have dispensed with his company, but had no decent excuse, as Tom's home lay in the same direction as his.

"Well, Randolph, you've won the watch," said Tom, when they were out of hearing of the other boys.

"Yes," answered Randolph, indifferently. "I don't care so much for that as for the ten dollars my father is going to give me."

"That's what I thought. You've got another watch, you know—more valuable."

"Well, what of it?" said Randolph, suspiciously.

"I think you might give me the Waterbury. I haven't got any."

"Why should I give it to you?" answered Randolph, coldly.

"Because but for me you wouldn't have won it, nor the ten dollars, neither."

"How do you make that out?"

"The teacher said so himself."

"I don't agree to it."

"You can't deny it. Luke was seven or eight rods ahead when I got in his way."

"Then it was lucky for me."

"It isn't lucky for me. My head hurts awfully."

"I'm very sorry, of course."

"That won't do me any good. Come, Randolph, give me the watch, like a good fellow."

"Well, you've got cheek, I must say. I want the watch myself."

"And is that all the satisfaction I am to get for my broken head?" exclaimed Tom, indignantly.

Randolph was a thoroughly mean boy, who, if he had had a dozen watches, would have wished to keep them all for himself.

"I've a great mind to tell Luke and the teacher of the arrangement between us."

"There wasn't any arrangement," said Randolph, sharply. "However, as I'm really sorry for you, I am willing to give you a quarter. There, now, don't let me hear any more about the matter."

He drew a silver quarter from his vest pocket and tendered it to Tom.

Tom Harper was not a sensitive boy, but his face flushed with indignation and shame, and he made no offer to take the money.

"Keep your quarter, Randolph Duncan," he said scornfully. "I think you're the meanest specimen of a boy that I ever came across. Any boy is a fool to be your friend. I don't care to keep company with you any longer."

"This to me!" exclaimed Randolph, angrily. "This is the pay I get for condescending to let you go with me."

"You needn't condescend any longer," said Tom, curtly, and he crossed to the other side of the street.

Randolph looked after him rather uneasily. After all, he was sorry to lose his humble follower.

"He'll be coming round in a day or two to ask me to take him back," he reflected. "I would be willing to give him ten cents more, but as for giving him the watch, he must think me a fool to part with that."

CHAPTER IV

LUKE'S NIGHT ADVENTURE

"I AM sorry you have lost the watch, Luke," said the teacher, after Randolph's departure. "You will have to be satisfied with deserving it."

"I am reconciled to the disappointment, sir," answered Luke. "I can get along for the present without a watch."

Nevertheless, Luke did feel disappointed. He had fully expected to have the watch to carry home and display to his mother. As it was, he was in no hurry to go home, but remained for two hours skating with the other boys. He used his friend Linton's skates, Linton having an engagement which prevented his remaining.

It was five o'clock when Luke entered the little cottage which he called home. His mother, a pleasant woman of middle age, was spreading the cloth for supper. She looked up as he entered.

"Well, Luke?" she said inquiringly.

"I haven't brought home the watch, mother," he said. "Randolph Duncan won it by accident. I will tell you about it."

After he had done so, Mrs. Larkin asked thoughtfully: "Isn't it a little singular that Tom should have got in your way?"

"Yes; I thought so at the time."

"Do you think there was any arrangement between him and Randolph?"

"As you ask me, mother, I am obliged to say that I do."

"It was a very mean trick!" said Mrs. Larkin, resentfully.

"Yes, it was; but poor Tom was well punished for it. Why, he's got a bunch on the back of his head almost as large as a hen's egg."

"I don't pity him," said Mrs. Larkin.

"I pity him, mother, for I don't believe Randolph will repay him for the service done him. If Randolph had met with the same accident I am not prepared to say that I should have pitied him much."

"You might have been seriously injured yourself, Luke."

"I might, but I wasn't, so I won't take that into consideration. However, mother, watch or no watch, I've got a good appetite. I shall be ready when supper is."

Luke sat down to the table ten minutes afterward and proved his words good, much to his mother's satisfaction.

While he is eating we will say a word about the cottage. It was small, containing only four rooms, furnished in the plainest fashion. The rooms, however, were exceedingly neat, and presented an appearance of comfort. Yet the united income of Mrs. Larkin and Luke was very small. Luke received a dollar a week for taking care of the schoolhouse, but this income only lasted forty weeks in the year. Then he did odd jobs for the neighbors, and picked up perhaps as much more. Mrs. Larkin had some skill as a dressmaker, but Groveton was a small village, and there was another in the same line, so that her income from this source probably did not average more than three dollars a week. This was absolutely all that they had to live on, though there was no rent to pay; and the reader will not be surprised to learn that Luke had no money to spend for watches.

"Are you tired, Luke?" asked his mother, after supper.

"No, mother. Can I do anything for you?"

"I have finished a dress for Miss Almira Clark. I suppose she will want to wear it to church tomorrow. But she lives so far away, I don't like to ask you to carry it to her."

"Oh, I don't mind. It won't do me any harm."

"You will get tired."

"If I do, I shall sleep the better for it."

"You are a good son, Luke."

"I ought to be. Haven't I got a good mother?"

So it was arranged. About seven o'clock, after his chores were done—for there was some wood to saw and split—Luke set out, with the bundle under his arm, for the house of Miss Clark, a mile and a half away.

It was a commonplace errand, that on which Luke had started, but it was destined to be a very important day in his life. It was to be a turning-point, and to mark the beginning of a new chapter of experiences. Was it to be for good or ill? That we are not prepared to reveal. It will be necessary for the reader to follow his career, step by step, and decide for himself.

Of course, Luke had no thought of this when he set out. To him it had been a marked day on account of the skating match, but this had turned out a disappointment. He accomplished his errand, which occupied a considerable time, and then set out on his return. It was half-past eight, but the moon had risen and diffused a mild radiance over the landscape. Luke thought he would shorten his homeward way by taking a path through the woods. It was not over a quarter of a mile, but would shorten the distance by as much more. The trees were not close together, so that it was light enough to see. Luke had nearly reached the edge of the wood, when he overtook a tall man, a stranger in the neighborhood, who carried in his hand a tin box. Turning, he eyed Luke sharply.

"Boy, what's your name?" he asked.

"Luke Larkin," our hero answered, in surprise.

"Where do you live?"

"In the village yonder."

"Will you do me a favor?"

"What is it, sir?"

"Take this tin box and carry it to your home. Keep it under lock and key till I call for it."

"Yes, sir, I can do that. But how shall I know you again?"

"Take a good look at me, that you may remember me."

"I think I shall know you again, but hadn't you better give me a name?"

"Well, perhaps so," answered the other, after a moment's thought. "You may call me Roland Reed. Will you remember?"

"Yes, sir."

"I am obliged to leave this neighborhood at once, and can't conveniently carry the box," explained the stranger. "Here's something for your trouble."

Luke was about to say that he required no money, when it occurred to him that he had no right to refuse, since money was so scarce at home. He took the tin box and thrust the bank-bill into his vest pocket. He wondered how much it was, but it was too dark to distinguish.

"Good night!" said Luke, as the stranger turned away.

"Good night!" answered his new acquaintance, abruptly.

If Luke could have foreseen the immediate consequences of this apparently simple act, and the position in which it would soon place him, he would certainly have refused to take charge of the box. And yet in so doing it might have happened that he had made a mistake. The consequences of even our simple acts are oftentimes far-reaching and beyond the power of human wisdom to foreknow.

Luke thought little of this as, with the box under his arm, he trudged homeward.

CHAPTER V

LUKE RECEIVES AN INVITATION

"WHAT have you there, Luke?" asked Mrs. Larkin, as Luke entered the little sitting-room with the tin box under his arm.

"I met a man on my way home, who asked me to keep it for him."

"Do you know the man?" asked his mother, in surprise.

"No," answered Luke.

"It seems very singular. What did he say?"

"He said that he was obliged to leave the neighborhood at once, and could not conveniently carry the box."

"Do you think it contains anything of value?"

"Yes, mother. It is like the boxes rich men have to hold their stocks and bonds. I was at the bank one day, and saw a gentleman bring in one to deposit in the safe."

"I can't understand that at all, Luke. You say you did not know this man?"

"I never met him before."

"And, of course, he does not know you?"

"No, for he asked my name."

"Yet he put what may be valuable property in your possession."

"I think," said Luke, shrewdly, "he had no one else to trust it to. Besides, a country boy wouldn't be very likely to make use of stocks and bonds."

"No, that is true. I suppose the tin box is locked?"

"Yes, mother. The owner—he says his name is Roland Reed—wishes it put under lock and key."

"I can lock it up in my trunk, Luke."

"I think that will be a good idea."

"I hope he will pay you for your trouble when he takes away the tin box."

"He has already; I forgot to mention it," and Luke drew from his vest pocket the bank-note he had thrust in as soon as received. "Why, it's a ten-dollar bill!" he exclaimed. "I wonder whether he knew he was giving me as much?"

"I presume so, Luke," said his mother, brightening up. "You are in luck!"

"Take it, mother. You will find a use for it."

"But, Luke, this money is yours."

"No, it is yours, for you are going to take care of the box."

It was, indeed, quite a windfall, and both mother and son retired to rest in a cheerful frame of mind, in spite of Luke's failure in the race.

"I have been thinking, Luke," said his mother, at the breakfast-table, "that I should like to have you buy a Waterbury watch out of this money. It will only cost three dollars and a half, and that is only one-third."

"Thank you, mother, but I can get along without the watch. I cared for it chiefly because it was to be a prize given to the best skater. All the boys know that I would have won but for the accident, and that satisfies me."

"I should like you to have a watch, Luke."

"There is another objection, mother. I don't want any one to know about the box or the money. If it were known that we had so much property in the house, some attempt might be made to rob us."

"That is true, Luke. But I hope it won't be long before you have a watch of your own."

When Luke was walking, after breakfast, he met Randolph Duncan, with a chain attached to the prize watch ostentatiously displayed on the outside of his vest. He smiled complacently, and rather triumphantly, when he met Luke. But Luke looked neither depressed nor angry.

"I hope your watch keeps good time, Randolph," he said.

"Yes; it hasn't varied a minute so far. I think it will keep as good time as my silver watch."

"You are fortunate to have two watches."

"My father has promised me a gold watch when I am eighteen," said Randolph, pompously.

"I don't know if I shall have any watch at all when I am eighteen."

"Oh, well, you are a poor boy. It doesn't matter to you."

"I don't know about that, Randolph. Time is likely to be of as much importance to a poor boy as to a rich boy."

"Oh, ah! yes, of course, but a poor boy isn't expected to wear a watch."

Here the conversation ended. Luke walked on with an amused smile on his face.

"I wonder how it would seem to be as complacent and self-satisfied as Randolph?" he thought. "On the whole, I would rather be as I am."

"Good morning, Luke!"

It was a girl's voice that addressed him. Looking up, he met the pleasant glance of Florence Grant, considered by many the prettiest girl in Groveton. Her mother was a widow in easy circumstances, who had removed from Chicago three years before, and occupied a handsome cottage nearly opposite Mr. Duncan's residence. She was a general favorite, not only for her good looks, but on account of her pleasant manner and sweet disposition.

"Good morning, Florence," said Luke, with an answering smile.

"What a pity you lost the race yesterday!"

"Randolph doesn't think so."

"No; he is a very selfish boy, I am afraid."

"Did you see the race?" asked Luke.

"No, but I heard all about it. If it hadn't been for Tom Harper you would have won, wouldn't you?"

"I think so."

"All the boys say so. What could have induced Tom to get in the way?"

"I don't know. It was very foolish, however. He got badly hurt."

"Tom is a friend of Randolph," said Florence significantly.

"Yes," answered Luke; "but I don't think Randolph would stoop to such a trick as that."

"You wouldn't, Luke, but Randolph is a different boy. Besides, I hear he was trying for something else."

"I know; his father offered him ten dollars besides."

"I don't see why it is that some fare so much better than

others," remarked Florence, thoughtfully. "The watch and the money would have done you more good."

"So they would, Florence, but I don't complain. I may be better off some day than I am now."

"I hope you will, Luke," said Florence, cordially.

"I am very much obliged to you for your good wishes," said Luke, warmly.

"That reminds me, Luke, next week, Thursday, is my birthday, and I am to have a little party in the evening. Will you come?"

Luke's face flushed with pleasure. Though he knew Florence very well from their being schoolfellows, he had never visited the house. He properly regarded the invitation as a compliment, and as a mark of friendship from one whose good opinion he highly valued.

"Thank you, Florence," he said. "You are very kind, and I shall have great pleasure in being present. Shall you have many?"

"About twenty. Your friend Randolph will be there."

"I think there will be room for both of us," said Luke, with a smile.

The young lady bade him good morning and went on her way.

Two days later Luke met Randolph at the dry-goods store in the village.

"What are you buying?" asked Randolph, condescendingly.

"Only a spool of thread for my mother."

"I am buying a new necktie to wear to Florence Grant's birthday party," said Randolph, pompously.

"I think I shall have to do the same," said Luke, enjoying the surprise he saw expressed on Randolph's face.

"Are you going?" demanded Randolph, abruptly.

"Yes."

"Have you been invited?"

"That is a strange question," answered Luke, indignantly. "Do you think I would go without an invitation?"

"Really, it will be quite a mixed affair," said Randolph, shrugging his shoulders.

"If you think so, why do you go?"

"I don't want to disappoint Florence."

Luke smiled. He was privately of the opinion that the disappointment wouldn't be intense.

CHAPTER VI

PREPARING FOR THE PARTY

THE evening of the party arrived. It was quite a social event at Groveton, and the young people looked forward to it with pleasant anticipation. Randolph went so far as to order a new suit for the occasion. He was very much afraid it would not be ready in time, but he was not to be disappointed. At five o'clock on Thursday afternoon it was delivered, and Randolph, when arrayed in it, surveyed himself with great satisfaction. He had purchased a handsome new necktie, and he reflected with pleasure that no boy present—not even Linton—would be so handsomely dressed as himself. He had a high idea of his personal consequence, but he was also of the opinion that "fine feathers make fine birds," and his suit was of fine cloth and stylish make.

"I wonder what the janitor will wear?" he said to himself, with a curl of the lip. "A pair of overalls, perhaps. They would be very appropriate, certainly."

This was just the question which was occupying Luke's mind. He did not value clothes as Randolph did, but he liked to look neat. Truth to tell, he was not very well off as to wardrobe. He had his every-day suit, which he wore to school, and a better suit, which he had worn for over a year. It was of mixed cloth, neat in appearance, though showing signs of wear; but there was one trouble. During the past year Luke had grown considerably, and his coat-sleeves were nearly two inches too short, and the legs of his trousers deficient quite as much. Nevertheless, he dressed himself, and he, too, surveyed himself, not before a pier-glass, but before the small mirror in the kitchen.

"Don't my clothes look bad, mother?" he asked anxiously.

"They are neat and clean, Luke," said his mother, hesitatingly.

"Yes, I know; but they are too small."

"You have been growing fast in the last year, Luke," said his mother, looking a little disturbed. "I suppose you are not sorry for that?"

"No," answered Luke, with a smile, "but I wish my coat and trousers had grown, too."

"I wish, my dear boy, I could afford to buy you a new suit."

"Oh, never mind, mother," said Luke, recovering his cheerfulness. "They will do for a little while yet. Florence didn't invite me for my clothes."

"No; she is a sensible girl. She values you for other reasons."

"I hope so, mother. Still, when I consider how handsomely Randolph will be dressed, I can't help thinking that there is considerable difference in our luck."

"Would you be willing to exchange with him, Luke?"

"There is one thing I wouldn't like to exchange."

"And what is that?"

"I wouldn't exchange my mother for his," said Luke, kissing the widow affectionately. "His mother is a cold, proud, disagreeable woman, while I have the best mother in the world."

"Don't talk foolishly, Luke," said Mrs. Larkin; but her face brightened, and there was a warm feeling in her heart, for it was very pleasant to her to hear Luke speak of her in this way.

"I won't think any more about it, mother," said Luke. "I've got a new necktie, at any rate, and I will make that do."

Just then there was a knock at the door, and Linton entered.

"I thought I would come round and go to the party with you, Luke," he said.

Linton was handsomely dressed, though he had not bought a suit expressly, like Randolph. He didn't appear to notice Luke's scant suit. Even if he had, he would have been too much of a gentleman to refer to it.

"I think we shall have a good time," he said. "We always do at Mrs. Grant's. Florence is a nice girl, and they know how to make it pleasant. I suppose we shall have dancing."

"I don't know how to dance," said Luke, regretfully. "I should like to have taken lessons last winter when Professor Bent had a class, but I couldn't afford it."

"You have seen dancing?"

"Oh, yes."

"It doesn't take much knowledge to dance a quadrille, particularly if you get on a side set. Come, we have an hour before it is time to go. Suppose I give you a lesson?"

"Do you think I could learn enough in that time to venture?"

"Yes, I do. If you make an occasional mistake it won't matter. So, if your mother will give us the use of the sitting-room, I will commence instructions."

Luke had looked at some dancers in the dining-room at the hotel, and was not wholly a novice, therefore. Linton was an excellent dancer, and was clear in his directions. It may also be said that Luke was a ready learner. So it happened at the end of the hour that the pupil had been initiated not only in the ordinary changes of the quadrille, but also in one contra dance, the Virginia Reel, which was a great favorite among the young people of Groveton.

"Now, I think you'll do, Luke," said Linton, when the lesson was concluded. "You are very quick to learn."

"You think I won't be awkward, Linton?"

"No, if you keep cool and don't get flustered."

"I am generally pretty cool. But I shall be rather surprised to see myself on the floor," laughed Luke.

"No doubt others will be, but you'll have a great deal more fun."

"So I shall. I don't like leaning against the wall while others are having a good time."

"If you could dance as well as you can skate you would have no trouble, Luke."

"No; that is where Randolph has the advantage of me."

"He is a very great dancer, though he can't come up to you in skating. However, dancing isn't everything. Dance as well as he may, he doesn't stand as high in the good graces of Florence Grant as he would like to do."

"I always noticed that he seemed partial to Florence."

"Yes, but it isn't returned. How about yourself, Luke?"

Luke, being a modest boy, blushed.

"I certainly think Florence a very nice girl," he said.

"I was sure of that," said Linton, smiling.

"But I don't want to stand in your way, Linton," continued Luke, with a smile.

"No danger, Luke. Florence is a year older than I am. Now, you are nearly two years older than she, and are better matched. So you needn't consider me in the matter."

Of course, this was all a joke. It was true, however, that of all the girls in Groveton, Luke was more attracted by Florence Grant than by any other, and they had always been excellent friends. It was well known that Randolph also was partial to the young lady, but he certainly had never received much encouragement.

Finally the boys got out, and were very soon at the door of

Mrs. Grant's handsome cottage. It was large upon the ground, with a broad veranda, in the Southern style. In fact, Mrs. Grant was Southern by birth, and, erecting the house herself, had it built after the fashion of her Southern birthplace.

Most of the young visitors had arrived when Luke and Linton put in an appearance. They had been detained longer than they were aware by the dancing-lesson.

Randolph and Sam Noble were sitting side by side at one end of the room, facing the entrance.

"Look," said Randolph, with a satirical smile, to his companion, "there comes the young janitor in his dress suit. Just look at his coat-sleeves and the legs of his trousers. They are at least two inches too short. Any other boy would be ashamed to come to a party in such ridiculous clothes."

Sam looked and tittered. Luke's face flushed, for, though he did not hear the words, he guessed their tenor. But he was made to forget them when Florence came forward and greeted Linton and himself with unaffected cordiality.

CHAPTER VII

FLORENCE GRANT'S PARTY

LUKE'S uncomfortable consciousness of his deficiencies in dress soon passed off. He noticed the sneer on Randolph's face and heard Sam's laugh, but he cared very little for the opinion of either of them. No other in the company appeared to observe his poor dress, and he was cordially greeted by them all, with the two exceptions already named.

"The janitor ought to know better than to intrude into the society of his superiors," said Randolph to Sam.

"He seems to enjoy himself," said Sam.

This was half an hour after the party had commenced, when all were engaged in one of the plays popular at a country party.

"I am going to have a party myself in a short time," continued Randolph, "but I shall be more select than Florence in my invitations. I shall not invite any working boys."

"Right you are, Randolph," said the subservient Sam. "I hope you won't forget me."

"Oh, no; I shall invite you. Of course, you don't move exactly in my circle, but, at any rate, you dress decently."

If Sam Noble had had proper pride he would have resented the insolent assumption of superiority in this speech, but he was content to play second fiddle to Randolph Duncan. His family, like himself, were ambitious to be on good terms with the leading families in the village, and did not mind an occasional snub.

"Shall you invite Tom Harper?" he asked.

He felt a little jealous of Tom, who had vied with him in flattering attentions to Randolph.

"No, I don't think so. Tom isn't here, is he?"

"He received an invitation, but ever since his accident he has been troubled with severe headaches, and I suppose that keeps him away."

"He isn't up to my standard," said Randolph, consequentially. "He comes of a low family."

"You and he have been together a good deal."

"Oh, I have found him of some service, but I have paid for it."

Yet this was the boy who, at his own personal risk, had obtained for Randolph the prize at the skating-match. Privately, Sam thought Randolph ungrateful, but he was, nevertheless, pleased at having distanced Tom in the favor of the young aristocrat.

After an hour, spent in various amusements, one of the company took her place at the piano, and dancing began.

"Now is your time, Luke," said Linton. "Secure a partner. It is only a quadrille."

"I feel a little nervous," said Luke. "Perhaps I had better wait till the second dance."

"Oh, nonsense! Don't be afraid."

Meanwhile, Randolph, with a great flourish, had invited Florence to dance.

"Thank you," she answered, taking his arm.

Randolph took his place with her as head couple. Linton and Annie Comray faced them. To Randolph's amazement, Luke and Fanny Pratt took their places as one of the side couples. Randolph, who was aware that Luke had never taken lessons, remarked this with equal surprise and disgust. His lip curled as he remarked to his partner: "Really, I didn't know that Luke Larkin danced."

"Nor I," answered Florence.

"I am sorry he is in our set."

"Why?" asked Florence, regarding him attentively.

"He will probably put us out by his clownish performance."

"Wouldn't it be well to wait and see whether he does or not?" responded Florence, quietly.

Randolph shrugged his shoulders.

"I pity his partner, at any rate," he said.

"I can't join in any such conversation about one of my guests," said Florence, with dignity.

Here the first directions were given, and the quadrille commenced.

Luke felt a little nervous, it must be confessed, and for that reason he watched with unusual care the movements of the head couples. He was quick to learn, and ordinarily cool and self-possessed. Besides, he knew that no one was likely to criticize him except Randolph. He saw the latter regarding him with a mocking smile, and this stimulated him to unusual carefulness. The result was that he went through his part with quite as much ease and correctness as any except the most practiced dancers. Florence said nothing, but she turned with a significant smile to Randolph. The latter looked disappointed and mortified. His mean disposition would have been gratified by Luke's failure, but this was a gratification he was not to enjoy.

The dance was at length concluded, and Luke, as he led his partner to a seat, felt that he had scored a success.

"May I have the pleasure of dancing with you next time, Florence?" asked Randolph.

"Thank you, but I should not think it right to slight my other guests," said the young lady.

Just then Luke came up and preferred the same request. He would not have done so if he had not acquitted himself well in the first quadrille.

Florence accepted with a smile.

"I was not aware that dancing was one of your accomplishments, Luke," she said.

"Nor I, till this evening," answered Luke. "There stands my teacher," and he pointed to Linton.

"You do credit to your teacher," said Florence. "I should not have known you were such a novice."

Luke was pleased with this compliment, and very glad that

he had been spared the mortification of breaking down before the eyes of his ill-wisher, Randolph Duncan. It is hardly necessary to say that he did equally well in the second quadrille, though he and Florence were head couple.

The next dance was the Virginia Reel. Here Florence had Linton for a partner, and Luke secured as his own partner a very good dancer. From prudence, however, he took his place at some distance from the head, and by dint of careful watching he acquitted himself as well as in the quadrilles.

"Really, Luke, you are doing wonderfully well," said Linton, when the dance was over. "I can hardly believe that you have taken but one lesson, and that from so poor a teacher as I am."

"I couldn't have had a better teacher, Lin," said Luke. "I owe my success to you."

"Didn't you say Luke couldn't dance?" asked Sam Noble of Randolph, later in the evening.

"He can't," answered Randolph, irritably.

"He gets along very well, I am sure. He dances as well as I do."

"That isn't saying much," answered Randolph, with a sneer. He could not help sneering even at his friends, and this was one reason why no one was really attached to him.

Sam walked away offended.

The party broke up at half-past ten. It was an early hour, but late enough considering the youth of the participants. Luke accompanied home one of the girls who had no brother present, and then turned toward his own home.

He had nearly reached it, when a tall figure, moving from the roadside, put a hand on his shoulder.

"You are Luke Larkin?" said the stranger, in questioning tone.

"Yes, sir."

"Is the tin box safe?"

"Yes, sir."

"That is all—for the present," and the stranger walked quickly away.

"Who can he be," thought Luke, in wonder, "and why should he have trusted a complete stranger—and a boy?"

Evidently there was some mystery about the matter. Had the stranger come honestly by the box, or was Luke aiding and abetting a thief? He could not tell.

CHAPTER VIII

MISS SPRAGUE DISCOVERS A SECRET

ABOUT this time it became known to one person in the village that the Larkins had in their possession a tin box, contents unknown.

This is the way it happened:

Among the best-known village residents was Miss Melinda Sprague, a maiden lady, who took a profound interest in the affairs of her neighbors. She seldom went beyond the limits of Groveton, which was her world. She had learned the business of dressmaking, and often did work at home for her customers. She was of a curious and prying disposition, and nothing delighted her more than to acquire the knowledge of a secret.

One day—a few days after Florence Grant's party—Mrs. Larkin was in her own chamber. She had the trunk open, having occasion to take something from it, when, with a light step, Miss Sprague entered the room. The widow, who was on her knees before the trunk, turning, recognized the intruder, not without displeasure.

"I hope you'll excuse my coming in so unceremoniously, Mrs. Larkin," said Melinda, effusively. "I knocked, but you didn't hear it, being upstairs, and I took the liberty, being as we were so well acquainted, to come upstairs in search of you."

"Yes, certainly," answered Mrs. Larkin, but her tone was constrained.

She quickly shut the lid of the trunk. There was only one thing among its contents which she was anxious to hide, but that Miss Melinda's sharp eyes had already discovered. Unfortunately, the tin box was at one side, in plain sight.

"What on earth does Mrs. Larkin do with a tin box?" she asked herself, with eager curiosity. "Can she have property that people don't know of? I always thought she was left poor."

Melinda asked no questions. The sudden closing of the trunk showed her that the widow would not be inclined to answer any questions.

"I won't let her think I saw anything," she said to herself. "Perhaps she'll get anxious and refer to it."

"We will go downstairs, Melinda," said Mrs. Larkin. "It will be more comfortable."

"If you have anything to do up here, I beg you won't mind me," said the spinster.

"No, I have nothing that won't wait."

So the two went down into the sitting-room.

"And how is Luke?" asked Miss Sprague, in a tone of friendly interest.

"Very well, thank you."

"Luke was always a great favorite of mine," continued the spinster. "Such a manly boy as he is!"

"He is a great help to me," said Mrs. Larkin.

"No doubt he is. He takes care of the schoolhouse, doesn't he?"

"Yes."

"How much pay does he get?"

"A dollar a week."

"I hope he will be able to keep the position."

"What do you mean, Melinda?" asked the widow, not without anxiety.

"You know Doctor Snodgrass has resigned on the school committee, and Squire Duncan has been elected in his place."

"Well?"

"Mrs. Flanagan went to him yesterday to ask to have her son Tim appointed janitor in place of Luke, and I heard that she received considerable encouragement from the squire."

"Do they find any fault with Luke?" asked Mrs. Larkin, jealously.

"No, not as I've heard; but Mrs. Flanagan said Luke had had it for a year, and now some one else ought to have the chance."

"Are you quite sure of this, Melinda?"

Miss Sprague, though over forty, was generally called by her first name, not as a tribute to her youth, but to the fact of her being still unmarried.

"Yes, I am; I had it from Mrs. Flanagan herself."

"I don't think Tim would do as well as Luke. He has never been able to keep a place yet."

"Just so; but, of course, his mother thinks him a polygon."

Probably Miss Sprague meant a paragon—she was not very careful in her speech, but Mrs. Larkin did not smile at her mistake. She was too much troubled at the news she had just heard. A dollar a week may seem a ridiculous trifle to some of my readers, but, where the entire income of the family was so small, it was a matter of some consequence.

"I don't think Luke has heard anything of this," said the widow. "He has not mentioned it to me."

"Perhaps there won't be any change, after all," said Melinda. "I am sure Tim Flanagan wouldn't do near as well as Luke."

Miss Melinda was not entirely sincere. She had said to Mrs. Flanagan that she quite agreed with her that Luke had been janitor long enough, and hoped Tim would get the place. She was in the habit of siding with the person she chanced to be talking with at the moment, and this was pretty well understood.

Luke, however, had heard of this threatened removal. For this, it may be said, Randolph was partly responsible. Just after Mrs. Flanagan's call upon the squire to solicit his official influence, Prince Duncan mentioned the matter to his son.

"How long has Luke Larkin been janitor at the schoolhouse?" he asked.

"About a year. Why do you ask?"

"Does he attend to the duties pretty well?"

"I suppose so. He's just fit to make fires and sweep the floor," answered Randolph, his lip curling.

"Mrs. Flanagan has been here to ask me to appoint her son Tim in Luke's place."

"You'd better do it, pa," said Randolph, quickly.

"Why? You say Luke is well fitted for the position."

"Oh, anybody could do as well, but Luke puts on airs. He feels too big for his position."

"I suppose Mrs. Larkin needs the money."

"So does Mrs. Flanagan," said Randolph.

"What sort of a boy is Tim? I have heard that he is lazy."

"Oh, I guess he'll do. Of course, I am not well acquainted with a boy like him," said the young aristocrat. "But I'm quite disgusted with Luke. He was at Florence Grant's party the other evening, and was cheeky enough to ask her to dance with him."

"Did she do so?"

"Yes; I suppose it was out of pity. He ought to have known better than to attend a party with such a suit. His coat and pantaloons were both too small for him, but he flourished around as if he were fashionably dressed."

Squire Duncan made no reply to his son's comments, but he

felt disposed, for reasons of his own, to appoint Tim Flanagan. He was hoping to be nominated for representative at the next election, and thought the appointment might influence the Irish vote in his favor.

"Shall you appoint Tim, pa?" asked Randolph.

"I think it probable. It seems only right to give him a chance. Rotation in office is a principle of which I approve."

"That's good!" thought Randolph, with a smile of gratification. "It isn't a very important place, but Luke will be sorry to lose it. The first time I see him I will give him a hint of it."

Randolph met Luke about an hour later in the village street. He did not often stop to speak with our hero, but this time he had an object in doing so.

CHAPTER IX

LUKE LOSES HIS POSITION

"LUKE LARKIN!"

Luke turned, on hearing his name called, and was rather surprised to see Randolph hastening toward him.

"How are you, Randolph?" he said politely.

"Where are you going?" asked Randolph, not heeding the inquiry.

"To the schoolhouse, to sweep out."

"How long have you been janitor?" asked Randolph, abruptly.

"About a year," Luke answered, in surprise.

"That's a good while."

Luke was puzzled. Why should Randolph feel such an interest, all at once, in his humble office?

"I suppose you know that my father is now on the school committee?" Randolph continued.

"Yes; I heard so."

"He thinks of appointing Tim Flanagan janitor in your place."

Luke's face showed his surprise and concern. The loss of his modest income would, as he knew, be severely felt by his mother and himself. The worst of it was, there seemed no chance in Groveton of making it up in any other way.

"Did your father tell you this?" he asked, after a pause.

"Yes; he just told me," answered Randolph, complacently.

"Why does he think of removing me? Are there any complaints of the way I perform my duties?"

"Really, my good fellow," said Randolph, languidly, "I can't enlighten you on that point. You've held the office a good while, you know."

"You are very kind to tell me—this bad news," said Luke, pointedly.

"Oh, don't mention it. Good morning. Were you fatigued after your violent exercise at Florence Grant's party?"

"No. Were you?"

"I didn't take any," said Randolph, haughtily. "I danced—I didn't jump round."

"Thank you for the compliment. Is there anything more you wish to say to me?"

"No."

"Then good morning."

When Luke was left alone he felt serious. How was he going to make up the dollar a week of which he was to be deprived? The more he considered the matter the further he was from thinking anything. He was not quite sure whether the news was reliable, or merely invented by Randolph to tease and annoy him. Upon this point, however, he was soon made certain. The next day, as he was attending to his duties in the schoolhouse, Tim Flanagan entered.

"Here's a note for you, Luke," he said.

Luke opened the note and found it brief but significant. It ran thus:

"LUKE LARKIN: I have appointed the bearer, Timothy Flanagan, janitor in your place. You will give him the key of the schoolhouse, and he will at once assume your duties.

"PRINCE DUNCAN."

"Well, Tim," said Luke, calmly, "it appears that you are going to take my place."

"Yes, Luke, but I don't care much about it. My mother went to the squire and got me the job. The pay's a dollar a week, isn't it?"

"Yes."

"That isn't enough."

"It isn't very much, but there are not many ways of earning money here in Groveton."

"What do you have to do?"

"Make the fire every morning and sweep out twice a week. Then there's dusting, splitting up kindlings, and so on."

"I don't think I'll like it. I ain't good at makin' fires."

"Squire Duncan writes you are to begin at once."

"Shure, I'm afraid I won't succeed."

"I'll tell you what, Tim. I'll help you along till you've got used to the duties. After a while they'll get easy for you."

"Will you now? You're a good feller, Luke. I thought you would be mad at losin' the job."

"I am not mad, but I am sorry. I needed the money, but no doubt you do, also. I have no grudge against you."

Luke had just started in his work. He explained to Tim how to do it, and remained with him till it was done.

"I'll come again to-morrow, Tim," he said. "I will get you well started, for I want to make it easy for you."

Tim was by no means a model boy, but he was warm-hearted, and he was touched by Luke's generous treatment.

"I say, Luke," he exclaimed, "I don't want to take your job. Say the word, and I'll tell mother and the squire I don't want it."

"No, Tim, it's your duty to help your mother. Take it and do your best."

On his way home Luke chanced to meet the squire, walking in his usual dignified manner toward the bank, of which he was president.

"Squire Duncan," he said, walking up to him in a manly way, "I would like to speak a word to you."

"Say on, young man."

"Tim Flanagan handed me a note from you this morning ordering me to turn over my duties as janitor to him."

"Very well?"

"I have done so, but I wish to ask you if I have been removed on account of any complaints that my work was not well done?"

"I have heard no complaints," answered the squire. "I appointed Timothy in your place because I approved of rotation in office. It won't do any good for you to make a fuss about it."

"I don't intend to make a fuss, Squire Duncan," said Luke, proudly. "I merely wished to know if there were any charges against me."

"There are none."

"Then I am satisfied. Good morning, sir."

"Stay, young man. Is Timothy at the schoolhouse?"

"Yes, sir. I gave him some instruction about the work, and promised to go over to-morrow to help him."

"Very well."

Squire Duncan was rather relieved to find that Luke did not propose to make any fuss. His motive, as has already been stated, was a political one. He wished to ingratiate himself with Irish voters and obtain an election as representative; not that he cared so much for this office, except as a stepping-stone to something higher.

Luke turned his steps homeward. He dreaded communicating the news to his mother, for he knew that it would depress her, as it had him. However, it must be known sooner or later, and he must not shrink from telling her.

"Mother," he said, as he entered the room where she was sewing, "I have lost my job as janitor."

"I expected you would, Luke," said his mother, soberly.

"Who told you?" asked Luke, in surprise.

"Melinda Sprague was here yesterday and told me Tim Flanagan was to have it."

"Miss Sprague seems to know everything that is going on."

"Yes, she usually hears everything. Have you lost the place already?"

"Tim brought me a note this morning from Squire Duncan informing me that I was removed and he was put in my place."

"It is going to be a serious loss to us, Luke," said Mrs. Larkin, gravely.

"Yes, mother, but I am sure something will turn up in its place."

Luke spoke confidently, but it was a confidence he by no means felt.

"It is a sad thing to be so poor as we are," said Mrs. Larkin, with a sigh.

"It is very inconvenient, mother, but we ought to be glad that we have perfect health. I am young and strong, and I am sure I can find some other way of earning a dollar a week."

"At any rate, we will hope so, Luke."

Luke went to bed early that night. The next morning, as they were sitting at breakfast, Melinda Sprague rushed into the house and sank into a chair, out of breath.

"Have you heard the news?"

"No. What is it?"

"The bank has been robbed! A box of United States bonds has been taken, amounting to thirty or forty thousand dollars!"

Luke and his mother listened in amazement.

CHAPTER X

MELINDA MAKES MISCHIEF

"WHERE did you hear this, Melinda?" asked Mrs. Larkin.

"I called on Mrs. Duncan just now—I was doing some work for her—and she told me. Isn't it awful?"

"Was the bank broken open last night, Miss Sprague?" asked Luke.

"I don't know when it was entered."

"I don't understand it at all," said Luke, looking puzzled.

"All I know is that, on examining the safe, the box of bonds was missing."

"Then it might have been taken some time since?"

"Yes, it might."

The same thought came to Luke and his mother at once. Was the mysterious stranger the thief, and had he robbed the bank and transferred the tin box to Luke? It might be so, but, as this happened more than a fortnight since, it would have been strange in that case that the box had not been missed sooner at the bank. Luke longed to have Miss Sprague go, that he might confer with his mother on this subject. He had been told to keep the possession of the box secret, and therefore he didn't wish to reveal the fact that he had it unless it should prove to be necessary.

"Were any traces of the robber discovered?" he added.

"Not that I heard of; but I pity the thief, whoever he is," remarked Melinda. "When he's found out he will go to jail, without any doubt."

"I can't understand, for my part, how an outside party could open the safe," said Mrs. Larkin. "It seems very mysterious."

"There's many things we can't understand," said Melinda, shaking her head sagely. "All crimes are mysterious."

"I hope they'll find out who took the bonds," said the widow. "Did they belong to the bank?"

"No, they belonged to a gentleman in Cavendish, who kept them in the bank, thinking they would be safer than in his own house. Little did he know what iniquity there was even in quiet country places like Groveton."

"Surely, Melinda, you don't think any one in Groveton robbed the bank?" said Mrs. Larkin.

"There's no knowing!" said Miss Sprague, solemnly. "There's those that we know well, or think we do, but we cannot read their hearts and their secret ways."

"Have you any suspicions, Miss Sprague?" asked Luke, considerably amused at the portentous solemnity of the visitor.

"I may and I may not, Luke," answered Melinda, with the air of one who knew a great deal more than she chose to tell; "but it isn't proper for me to speak at present."

Just then Miss Sprague saw some one passing who, she thought, had not heard of the robbery, and, hastily excusing herself, she left the house.

"What do you think, Luke?" asked his mother, after the spinster had gone. "Do you think the box we have was taken from the bank?"

"No, I don't, mother. I did think it possible at first, but it seems very foolish for the thief, if he was one, to leave the box in the same village, in the charge of a boy. It would have been more natural and sensible for him to open it, take out the bonds, and throw it away or leave it in the woods."

"There is something in that," said Mrs. Larkin, thoughtfully. "There is certainly a mystery about our box, but I can't think it was stolen from the bank."

Meanwhile, Miss Sprague had formed an important resolve. The more she thought of it, the more she believed the missing box was the one of which she had caught a glimpse of in Mrs. Larkin's trunk. True, Luke and the widow had not betrayed that confusion and embarrassment which might have been anticipated when the theft was announced, but she had noticed the look exchanged between them, and she was sure it meant something. Above all, her curiosity was aroused to learn how it happened that a woman as poor as the Widow Larkin should have a tin box in her trunk, the contents of which might be presumed to be valuable.

"I don't like to get Luke and his mother into trouble," Melinda said to herself, "but I think it my duty to tell all I know. At any rate, they will have to tell how the box came into their possession, and what it contains. I'll go to the bank and speak to Squire Duncan."

Prince Duncan had called an extra meeting of the directors to consider the loss which had been discovered, and they were now seated in the bank parlor. There were three of them present, all of whom resided in Groveton—Mr. Manning, the hotelkeeper; Mr. Bailey, a storekeeper, and Mr. Beane, the Groveton lawyer.

Miss Sprague entered the bank and went up to the little window presided over by the paying-teller.

"Is Squire Duncan in the bank?" she asked.

"Yes, Miss Sprague."

"I would like to speak with him."

"That is impossible. He is presiding at a directors' meeting."

"Still, I would like to see him," persisted Melinda.

"You will have to wait," said the paying-teller, coldly. He had no particular respect or regard for Miss Sprague, being quite familiar with her general reputation as a gossip and busybody.

"I think he would like to see me," said Melinda, nodding her head with mysterious significance. "There has been a robbery at the bank, hasn't there?"

"Do you know anything about it, Miss Sprague?" demanded the teller, in surprise.

"Maybe I do, and maybe I don't; but I've got a secret to tell to Squire Duncan."

"I don't believe it amounts to anything," thought the teller. "Well, I will speak to Squire Duncan," he said aloud.

He went to the door of the directors' room, and after a brief conference with Prince Duncan he returned with the message, "You may go in, Miss Sprague."

She nodded triumphantly, and with an air of conscious importance walked to the bank parlor.

Prince Duncan and his associates were sitting round a mahogany table.

Melinda made a formal curtsy and stood facing them.

"I understand, Miss Sprague, that you have something to communicate to us in reference to the loss the bank has just sustained," said the squire, clearing his throat.

"I thought it my duty to come and tell you all I knew, Squire Duncan and gentlemen," said Melinda.

"Quite right, Miss Sprague. Now, what can you tell us?"

"The article lost was a tin box, was it not?"

"Yes."

"About so long?" continued Miss Sprague, indicating a length of about fifteen inches.

"Yes."

"What was there in it?"

"Government bonds."

"I know where there is such a box," said Miss Sprague, slowly.

"Where? Please be expeditious, Miss Sprague."

"A few days since I was calling on Mrs. Larkin—Luke's mother—just happened in, as I may say, and, not finding her downstairs, went up into her chamber. I don't think she heard me, for when I entered the chamber and spoke to her she seemed quite flustered. She was on her knees before an open trunk, and in that trunk I saw the tin box."

The directors looked at each other in surprise, and Squire Duncan looked undeniably puzzled.

"I knew the box was one such as is used to hold valuable papers and bonds," proceeded Melinda, "and, as I had always looked on the widow as very poor, I didn't know what to make of it."

"Did you question Mrs. Larkin about the tin box?" asked Mr. Beane.

"No; she shut the trunk at once, and I concluded she didn't want me to see it."

"Then you did not say anything about it?"

"No; but I went in just now to tell her about the bank being robbed."

"How did it seem to affect her?" asked Mr. Bailey.

"She and Luke—Luke was there, too—looked at each other in dismay. It was evident that they were thinking of the box in the trunk."

Melinda continued her story, and the directors were somewhat impressed.

"I propose," said Mr. Manning, "that we get out a search-warrant and search Mrs. Larkin's cottage. That box may be the one missing from the bank."

CHAPTER XI

LUKE IS ARRESTED

JUST after twelve o'clock, when Luke was at home eating dinner, a knock was heard at the front door.

"I'll go, mother," said Luke, and he rose from the table, and, going into the entry, opened the outer door.

His surprise may be imagined when he confronted Squire Duncan and the gentlemen already mentioned as directors of the Groveton bank.

"Did you wish to see mother?" he asked.

"Yes; we have come on important business," said Squire Duncan, pompously.

"Walk in, if you please."

Luke led the way into the little sitting-room, followed by the visitors. The dinner-table was spread in the kitchen adjoining. The room looked very much filled up with the unwonted company, all being large men.

"Mother," called Luke, "here are some gentlemen who wish to see you."

The widow entered the room, and looked with surprise from one to another. All waited for Squire Duncan, as the proper person, from his official position, to introduce the subject of their visit.

"Mrs. Larkin," said the squire, pompously, "it has possibly come to your ears that the Groveton Bank, of which you are aware that I am the president, has been robbed of a box of bonds?"

"Yes, sir. I was so informed by Miss Melinda Sprague this morning."

"I am also informed that you have in your custody a tin box similar to the one that has been taken."

He expected to see Mrs. Larkin show signs of confusion, but she answered calmly: "I have a box in my custody, but whether it resembles the one lost I can't say."

"Ha! you admit that you hold such a box?" said the squire, looking significantly at his companions.

"Certainly. Why should I not?"

"Are you willing to show it to us?"

"Yes, we are willing to show it," said Luke, taking it upon himself to answer, "but I have no idea that it will do you any good."

"That is for us to decide, young man," said Squire Duncan.

"Do you suppose it is the box missing from the bank, sir?"

"It may be."

"When did you miss the box?"

"Only this morning, but it may have been taken a month ago."

"This box has been in our possession for a fortnight."

"Such is your statement, Luke."

"It is the truth," said Luke, flushing with indignation.

"My boy," said Mr. Beane, "don't be angry. I, for one, have no suspicion that you have done anything wrong, but it is our duty to inquire into this matter."

"Who told you that we had such a box, Mr. Beane?"

"Miss Melinda Sprague was the informant."

"I thought so, mother," said Luke. "She is a prying old maid, and it is just like her."

"Miss Sprague only did her duty," said the squire. "But we are losing time. We require you to produce the box."

"I will get it, gentlemen," said the widow, calmly.

While she was upstairs, Mr. Manning inquired: "Where did you get the box, Luke?"

"If you identify it as the box taken from the bank," answered Luke, "I will tell you. Otherwise I should prefer to say nothing, for it is a secret of another person."

"Matters look very suspicious, in my opinion, gentlemen," said Squire Duncan, turning to his associates.

"Not necessarily," said Mr. Beane, who seemed inclined to favor our hero. "Luke may have a good reason for holding his tongue."

Here Mrs. Larkin presented herself with the missing box. Instantly it became an object of attention.

"It looks like the missing box," said the squire.

"Of course, I can offer no opinion," said Mr. Beane, "not having seen the one lost. Such boxes, however, have a general resemblance to each other."

"Have you the key that opens it?" asked the squire.

"No, sir."

"Squire Duncan," asked Mr. Beane, "have you the key unlocking the missing box?"

"No, sir," answered Squire Duncan, after a slight pause.

"Then I don't think we can decide as to the identity of the two boxes."

The trustees looked at each other in a state of indecision. No one knew what ought to be done.

"What course do you think we ought to take, Squire Duncan?" asked Mr. Bailey.

"I think," said the bank president, straightening up, "that there is sufficient evidence to justify the arrest of this boy Luke."

"I have done nothing wrong, sir," said Luke, indignantly. "I am no more of a thief than you are."

"Do you mean to insult me, you young jackanapes?" demanded Mr. Duncan, with an angry flush on his face.

"I intend to insult no one, but I claim that I have done nothing wrong."

"That is what all criminals say," sneered the squire.

Luke was about to make an angry reply, but Mr. Beane, waving his hand as a signal for our hero to be quiet, remarked calmly: "I think, Duncan, in justice to Luke, we ought to hear his story as to how the box came into his possession."

"That is my opinion," said Mr. Bailey. "I don't believe Luke is a bad boy."

Prince Duncan felt obliged to listen to that suggestion, Mr. Bailey and Mr. Beane being men of consideration in the village.

"Young man," he said, "we are ready to hear your story. From whom did you receive this box?"

"From a man named Roland Reed," answered Luke.

The four visitors looked at each other in surprise.

"And who is Roland Reed?" asked the president of the bank. "It seems very much like a fictitious name."

"It may be, for aught I know," said Luke, "but it is the name given me by the person who gave me the box to keep for him."

"State the circumstances," said Mr. Beane.

"About two weeks since I was returning from the house of Miss Almira Clark, where I had gone on an errand for my mother. To shorten my journey, I took my way through the woods. I had nearly passed through to the other side, when a tall man, dark complexioned, whom I had never seen before stepped up to me. He asked me my name, and, upon my telling him, asked if I would do him a favor. This was to take charge of a tin box, which he carried under his arm."

"The one before us?" asked Mr. Manning.

"Yes, sir."

"Did he give any reason for making this request?"

"He said he was about to leave the neighborhood, and wished it taken care of. He asked me to put it under lock and key."

"Did he state why he selected you for this trust?" asked Mr. Beane.

"No, sir; he paid me for my trouble, however. He gave me a bank-note, which, when I reached home, I found to be a ten-dollar bill."

"And you haven't seen him since?"

"Once only."

"When was that?"

"On the evening of Florence Grant's party. On my way home the same man came up to me and asked if the box was safe. I answered, 'Yes.' He said, 'That is all—for the present,' and disappeared. I have not seen him since."

"That is a very pretty romance," said Prince Duncan, with a sneer.

"I can confirm it," said Mrs. Larkin, calmly. "I saw Luke bring in the box, and at his request I took charge of it. The story he told at that time is the same that he tells now."

"Very possibly," said the bank president. "It was all cut and dried."

"You seem very much prejudiced against Luke," said Mrs. Larkin, indignantly.

"By no means, Mrs. Larkin. I judge him and his story from the standpoint of common sense. Gentlemen, I presume this story makes the same impression on you as on me?"

Mr. Beane shook his head. "It may be true; it is not impossible," he said.

"You believe, then, there is such a man as Roland Reed?"

"There may be a man who calls himself such."

"If there is such a man, he is a thief."

"It may be so, but that does not necessarily implicate Luke."

"He would be a receiver of stolen property."

"Not knowing it to be such."

"At all events, I feel amply justified in causing the arrest of Luke Larkin on his own statement."

"Surely you don't mean this?" exclaimed Mrs. Larkin, in dismay.

"Don't be alarmed, mother," said Luke, calmly. "I am innocent of wrong, and no harm will befall me."

CHAPTER XII

LUKE AS A PRISONER

PRINCE DUNCAN, who was a magistrate, directed the arrest of Luke on a charge of robbing the Groveton Bank. The constable who was called upon to make the arrest performed the duty unwillingly.

"I don't believe a word of it, Luke," he said. "It's perfect nonsense to say you have robbed the bank. I'd as soon believe myself guilty."

Luke was not taken to the lock-up, but was put in the personal custody of Constable Perkins, who undertook to be responsible for his appearance at the trial.

"You mustn't run away, or you'll get me into trouble, Luke," said the good-natured constable.

"It's the last thing I'd be willing to do, Mr. Perkins," said Luke, promptly. "Then everybody would decide that I was guilty. I am innocent, and want a chance to prove it."

What was to be done with the tin box, was the next question.

"I will take it over to my house," said Squire Duncan.

"I object," said Mr. Beane.

"Do you doubt my integrity?" demanded the bank president, angrily.

"No; but it is obviously improper that any one of us should take charge of the box before it has been opened and its contents examined. We are not even certain that it is the one missing from the bank."

As Mr. Beane was a lawyer, Prince Duncan, though unwillingly, was obliged to yield. The box, therefore, was taken to the bank and locked up in the safe till wanted.

It is hardly necessary to say that the events at the cottage of Mrs. Larkin, and Luke's arrest, made a great sensation in the village. The charge that Luke had robbed the bank was received not only with surprise, but with incredulity. The boy was so well and so favorably known in Groveton that few could be found to credit the charge. There were exceptions, however. Melinda Sprague enjoyed the sudden celebrity she had achieved as the original discoverer of the thief who had plundered the bank. She was inclined to believe that Luke was guilty, because it enhanced her own importance.

"Most people call Luke a good boy," she said, "but there was always something about him that made me suspicious.

"There was something in his expression—I can't tell you what—that set me to thinkin' all wasn't right. Appearances are deceitful, as our old minister used to say."

"They certainly are, if Luke is a bad boy and a thief," retorted the other, indignantly. "You might be in better business, Melinda, than trying to take away the character of a boy like Luke."

"I only did my duty," answered Melinda, with an air of superior virtue. "I had no right to keep secret what I knew about the robbery."

"You always claimed to be a friend of the Larkins. Only last week you took tea there."

"That's true. I am a friend now, but I can't consent to cover up inquiry. Do you know whether the bank has offered any reward for the detection of the thief?"

"No," said the other, shortly, with a look of contempt at the eager spinster. "Even if it did, and poor Luke were found guilty, it would be blood-money that no decent person would accept."

"Really, Mrs. Clark, you have singular ideas," said the discomfited Melinda. "I ain't after no money. I only mean to do my duty, but if the bank should recognize the value of my services, it would be only right and proper."

There was another who heard with great satisfaction of Luke's arrest. This was Randolph Duncan. As it happened, he was late in learning that his rival had got into trouble, not having seen his father since breakfast.

"This is great news about Luke," said his friend Sam Noble, meeting him on the street.

"What news? I have heard nothing," said Randolph, eagerly.

"He has been arrested."

"You don't say so!" exclaimed Randolph. "What has he done?"

"Robbed the bank of a tin box full of bonds. It was worth an awful lot of money."

"Well, well!" ejaculated Randolph. "I always thought he was a boy of no principle."

"The tin box was found in his mother's trunk."

"What did Luke say? Did he own up?"

"No; he brazened it out. He said the box was given him to take care of by some mysterious stranger."

"That's too thin. How was it traced to Luke?"

"It seems Old Maid Sprague"—it was lucky for Melinda's peace of mind that she did not hear this contemptuous reference to her—"went to the Widow Larkin's house one day and saw the tin box in her trunk."

"She didn't leave the trunk open, did she?"

"No; but she had it open, looking into it, when old Melinda crept upstairs softly and caught her at it."

"I suppose Luke will have to go to State's prison," said Randolph, with a gratified smile.

"I hope it won't be quite so bad as that," said Sam, who was not equal in malice to his aristocratic friend.

"I haven't any pity for him," said Randolph, decidedly. "If he chooses to steal, he must expect to be punished."

Just then Mr. Hooper, the grammer-school teacher, came up.

"Mr. Hooper," said Randolph, eagerly, "have you heard about Luke?"

"I have heard that he has been removed from his janitorship, and I'm sorry for it."

"If he goes to jail he wouldn't be able to be janitor," said Randolph.

"Goes to jail! What do you mean?" demanded the teacher, sharply.

Hereupon Randolph told the story, aided and assisted by Sam Noble, to whom he referred as his authority.

"This is too ridiculous!" said Mr. Hooper, contemptuously. "Luke is no thief, and if he had the tin box he has given the right explanation of how he came by it."

"I know he is a favorite of yours, Mr. Hooper, but that won't save him from going to jail," said Randolph, tartly.

"If he is a favorite of mine," said the teacher, with dignity, "it is for a very good reason. I have always found him to be a high-minded, honorable boy, and I still believe him to be so, in spite of the grave accusation that has been brought against him."

There was something in the teacher's manner that deterred Randolph from continuing his malicious attack upon Luke. Mr. Hooper lost no time in inquiring into the facts of the case, and then in seeking out Luke, whom he found in the constable's house.

"Luke," he said, extending his hand, "I have heard that you were in trouble, and I have come to see what I can do for you."

"You are very kind, Mr. Hooper," said Luke, gratefully. "I hope you don't believe me guilty."

"I would as soon believe myself guilty of the charge, Luke."

"That's just what I said, Mr. Hooper," said Constable Perkins. "Just as if there wasn't more than one tin box in the world."

"You never told any one that you had a tin box in your custody, I suppose, Luke?"

"No, sir; the man who asked me to take care of it especially cautioned me to say nothing about it."

"What was his name?"

"Roland Reed."

"Do you know where to find him? It would be of service to you if you could obtain his evidence. It would clear you at once."

"I wish I could, sir, but I have no idea where to look for him."

"That is unfortunate," said the teacher, knitting his brows in perplexity. "When are you to be brought to trial?"

"To-morrow, I hear."

"Well, Luke, keep up a good heart and hope for the best."

"I mean to, sir."

CHAPTER XIII

IN THE COURT-ROOM

IT WAS decided that Luke should remain until his trial in the personal custody of Constable Perkins. Except for the name of it, his imprisonment was not very irksome, for the Perkins family treated him as an honored guest, and Mrs. Perkins prepared a nicer supper than usual. When Mr. Perkins went out he said to his wife, with a quizzical smile: "I leave Luke in your charge. Don't let him run away."

"I'll look out for that," said Mrs. Perkins, smiling.

"Perhaps I had better leave you a pistol, my dear?"

"I am afraid I should not know how to use it."

"You might tie my hands," suggested Luke.

"That wouldn't prevent your walking away."

"Then my feet."

"It won't be necessary, husband," said Mrs. Perkins. "I've got the poker and tongs ready."

But, though treated in this jesting manner, Luke could not help feeling a little anxious. For aught he knew, the tin box taken from his mother's trunk might be the same which had been stolen from the bank. In that case Roland Reed was not likely to appear again, and his story would be disbelieved. It was a strange one, he could not help admitting to himself. Yet he could not believe that the mysterious stranger was a burglar. If he were, it seemed very improbable that he would have left his booty within half a mile of the bank, in the very village where the theft had been committed. It was all very queer, and he could not see into the mystery.

"I should like to do something," thought Luke. "It's dull work sitting here with folded hands."

"Isn't there something I can do, Mrs. Perkins?" he said. "I am not used to sitting about the house idle."

"Well, you might make me some pies," said Mrs. Perkins.

"You'd never eat them if I did. I can boil eggs and fry potatoes. Isn't there some wood to saw and split?"

"Plenty out in the shed."

"I understand that, at any rate. Have you any objection to my setting to work?"

"No, if you won't run away."

"Send out Charlie to watch me."

Charlie was a youngster about four years of age, and very fond of Luke, who was a favorite with most young children.

"Yes, that will do. Charlie, go into the shed and see Luke saw wood."

"Yes, mama."

"Don't let him run away."

"No, I won't," said Charlie, gravely.

Luke felt happier when he was fairly at work. It took his mind off his troubles, as work generally does, and he spent a couple of hours in the shed. Then Mrs. Perkins came to the door and called him.

"Luke," she said, "a young lady has called to see the prisoner."

"A young lady! Who is it?"

"Florence Grant."

Luke's face brightened up with pleasure; he put on his coat and went into the house.

"Oh, Luke, what a shame!" exclaimed Florence, hastening to him with extended hand. "I only just heard of it."

"Then you're not afraid to shake hands with a bank burglar?" said Luke.

"No, indeed! What nonsense it is! Who do you think told me of your arrest?"

"Randolph Duncan."

"You have guessed it."

"What did he say? Did he seem to be shocked at my iniquity?"

"I think he seemed glad of it. Of course, he believes you guilty."

"I supposed he would, or pretend to, at any rate. I think his father is interested to make me out guilty. I hope you don't think there is any chance of it?"

"Of course not, Luke. I know you too well. I'd sooner suspect Randolph. He wanted to know what I thought of you now."

"And what did you answer?"

"That I thought the same as I always had—that you were one of the best boys in the village. 'I admire your taste,' said Randolph, with a sneer. Then I gave him a piece of my mind."

"I should like to have heard you, Florence."

"I don't know; you have no idea what a virago I am when I am mad. Now sit down and tell me all about it."

Luke obeyed, and the conversation was a long one, and seemed interesting to both. In the midst of it Linton Tomkins came in.

"Have you come to see the prisoner, also, Linton?" asked Florence.

"Yes, Florence. What a desperate-looking ruffian he is! I don't dare to come too near. How did you break into the bank, Luke?"

First Luke smiled, then he became grave. "After all, it is no joke to me, Linny," he said. "Think of the disgrace of being arrested on such a charge."

"The disgrace is in being a burglar, not in being arrested for one, Luke. Of course, it's absurd. Father wants me to say that if you are bound over for trial he will go bail for you to any amount."

"Your father is very kind, Linny. I may need to avail myself of his kindness."

The next day came, and at ten o'clock, Luke, accompanied by Constable Perkins, entered the room in which Squire Duncan sat as trial justice. A considerable number of persons were gathered, for it was a trial in which the whole village was interested. Among them was Mrs. Larkin, who wore an anxious, perturbed look.

"Oh, Luke," she said sorrowfully, "how terrible it is to have you here!"

"Don't be troubled, mother," said Luke. "We both know that I am innocent, and I rely on God to stand by me."

"Luke," said Mr. Beane, "though I am a bank trustee, I am your friend and believe you innocent. I will act as your lawyer."

"Thank you, Mr. Beane. I shall be very glad to accept your services."

The preliminary proceedings were of a formal character. Then Miss Melinda Sprague was summoned to testify. She professed to be very unwilling to say anything likely to injure her good friends, Luke and his mother, but managed to tell, quite dramatically, how she first caught a glimpse of the tin box.

"Did Mrs. Larkin know that you saw it?" asked the squire.

"She didn't know for certain," answered Melinda, "but she was evidently afraid I would, for she shut the trunk in a hurry, and seemed very much confused. I thought of this directly when I heard of the bank robbery, and I went over to tell Luke and his mother."

"How did they receive your communication?"

"They seemed very much frightened."

"And you inferred that they had not come honestly by the tin box?"

"It grieves me to say that I did," said Melinda, putting her handkerchief to her eyes to brush away an imaginary tear.

Finally Melinda sat down, and witnesses were called to testify to Luke's good character. There were more who wished to be sworn than there was time to hear. Mr. Beane called only Mr. Hooper, Mr. Tomkins and Luke's Sunday-school teacher. Then he called Luke to testify in his own defense.

Luke told a straightforward story—the same that he had told before—replying readily and easily to any questions that were asked him.

"I submit, Squire Duncan," said Mr. Beane, "that my client's statement is plain and frank and explains everything. I hold that it exonerates him from all suspicion of complicity with the robbery."

"I differ with you," said Squire Duncan, acidly. "It is a wild, improbable tale, that does not even do credit to the prisoner's invention. In my opinion, this mysterious stranger has no existence. Is there any one besides himself who has seen this Roland Reed?"

At this moment there was a little confusion at the door. A tall, dark-complexioned stranger pushed his way into the courtroom. He advanced quickly to the front.

"I heard my name called," he said. "There is no occasion to doubt my existence. I am Roland Reed!"

CHAPTER XIV

AN IMPORTANT WITNESS

THE effect of Roland Reed's sudden appearance in the courtroom, close upon the doubt expressed as to his existence, was electric. Every head was turned, and every one present looked with eager curiosity at the mysterious stranger. They saw a dark-complexioned, slender, but wiry man, above the middle height, with a pair of keen black eyes scanning, not without sarcastic amusement, the faces turned toward him.

Luke recognized him at once.

"Thank God!" he ejaculated, with a feeling of intense relief. "Now my innocence will be made known."

Squire Duncan was quite taken aback. His face betrayed his surprise and disappointment.

"I don't know you," he said, after a pause.

"Perhaps not, Mr. Duncan," answered the stranger, in a significant tone, "but I know you."

"Were you the man who gave this tin box to the defendant?"

"Wouldn't it be well, since this is a court, to swear me as a witness?" asked Roland Reed, quietly.

"Of course, of course," said the squire, rather annoyed to be reminded of his duty by this stranger.

This being done, Mr. Beane questioned the witness in the interest of his client.

"Do you know anything about the tin box found in the possession of Luke Larkin?" he asked.

"Yes, sir."

"Did you commit it to his charge for safe-keeping?"

"I did."

"Were you previously acquainted with Luke?"

"I was not."

"Was it not rather a singular proceeding to commit what is presumably of considerable value to an unknown boy?"

"It would generally be considered so, but I do many strange things. I had seen the boy by daylight, though he had never seen me, and I was sure I could trust him."

"Why, if you desired a place of safe-keeping for your box, did you not select the bank vaults?"

Roland Reed laughed, and glanced at the presiding justice.

"It might have been stolen," he said.

"Does the box contain documents of value?"

"The contents are valuable to me, at any rate."

"Mr. Beane," said Squire Duncan, irritably, "I think you are treating the witness too indulgently. I believe this box to be the one taken from the bank."

"You heard the remark of the justice," said the lawyer. "Is this the box taken from the bank?"

"It is not," answered the witness, contemptuously, "and no one knows this better than Mr. Duncan."

The justice flushed angrily.

"You are impertinent, witness," he said. "It is all very well to claim this box as yours, but I shall require you to prove ownership."

"I am ready to do so," said Roland Reed, quietly. "Is that the box on the table?"

"It is."

"Has it been opened?"

"No; the key has disappeared from the bank."

"The key is in the hands of the owner, where it properly belongs. With the permission of the court, I will open the box."

"I object," said Squire Duncan, quickly.

"Permit me to say that your refusal is extraordinary," said

Mr. Beane, pointedly. "You ask the witness to prove property, and then decline to allow him to do so."

Squire Duncan, who saw that he had been betrayed into a piece of folly, said sullenly: "I don't agree with you, Mr. Beane, but I withdraw my objection. The witness may come forward and open the box, if he can."

Roland Reed bowed slightly, advanced to the table, took a bunch of keys from his pocket, and inserting one of the smallest in the lock easily opened the box.

Those who were near enough, including the justice, craned their necks forward to look into the box.

The box contained papers, certificates of stock, apparently, and a couple of bank-books.

"The box missing from the vault contained government bonds, as I understand, Squire Duncan?" said the lawyer.

"Yes," answered the justice, reluctantly.

"Are there any government bonds in the box, Mr. Reed."

"You can see for yourself, sir."

The manner of the witness toward the lawyer was courteous, though in the tone in which he addressed the court there had been a scarcely veiled contempt.

"I submit, then, that my young client has been guilty of no wrong. He accepted the custody of the box from the rightful owner, and this he had a clear right to do."

"How do you know that the witness is the rightful owner of the box?" demanded the justice, in a cross tone. "He may have stolen it from some other quarter."

"There is not a shadow of evidence of this," said the lawyer, in a tone of rebuke.

"I am not sure but that he ought to be held."

"You will hold me at your peril, Mr. Duncan," said the witness, in clear, resolute tones. "I have a clear comprehension of my rights, and I do not propose to have them infringed."

Squire Duncan bit his lips. He had only a smattering of law, but he knew that the witness was right, and that he had been betrayed by temper into making a discreditable exhibition of himself.

"I demand that you treat me with proper respect," he said angrily.

"I am ready to do that," answered the witness, in a tone whose meaning more than one understood. It was not an apology calculated to soothe the ruffled pride of the justice.

"I call for the discharge of my young client, Squire Duncan," said the lawyer. "The case against him, as I hardly need say, has utterly failed."

"He is discharged," said the justice, unwillingly.

Instantly Luke's friends surrounded him and began to shower congratulations upon him. Among them was Roland Reed.

"My young friend," he said, "I am sincerely sorry that by any act of mine I have brought anxiety and trouble upon you. But I can't understand how the fact that you had the box in your possession became known."

This was explained to him.

"I have a proposal to make to you and your mother," said Roland Reed, "and with your permission I will accompany you home."

"We shall be glad to have you, sir," said Mrs. Larkin, cordially.

As they were making their way out of the court-room, Melinda Sprague, the cause of Luke's trouble, hurried to meet them. She saw by this time that she had made a great mistake, and that her course was likely to make her generally unpopular. She hoped to make it up with the Larkins.

"I am so glad you are acquitted, Luke," she began effusively. "I hope, Mrs. Larkin, you won't take offense at what I did. I did what I thought to be my duty, though with a bleeding heart. No one is more rejoiced at dear Luke's vindication."

"Miss Sprague," said she, "if you think you did your duty, let the consciousness of that sustain you. I do not care to receive any visits from you hereafter."

"How cruel and unfeeling you are, Mrs. Larkin," said the spinster, putting her handkerchief to her eyes.

Mrs. Larkin did not reply.

Miss Sprague found herself so coldly treated in the village that she shortly left Groveton on a prolonged visit to some relatives in a neighboring town. It is to be feared that the consciousness of having done her duty did not wholly console her. What she regretted most, however, was the loss of the reward which she had hoped to receive from the bank.

CHAPTER XV

THE LARKINS ARE IN LUCK

LUKE and his mother, accompanied by Roland Reed, took their way from the court-room to the widow's modest cottage.

"You may take the tin box, Luke," said the stranger, "if you are not afraid to keep in your charge what has given you so much trouble."

"All's well that ends well!" said Luke.

"Yes; I don't think it will occasion you any further anxiety."

Roland Reed walked in advance with Mrs. Larkin, leaving Luke to follow.

"What sort of a man is this Mr. Duncan?" he asked abruptly.

"Squire Duncan?"

"Yes, if that is his title."

"He is, upon the whole, our foremost citizen," answered the widow, after a slight hesitation.

"Is he popular?"

"I can hardly say that."

"He is president of the bank, is he not?"

"Yes."

"How long has he lived in Groveton?"

"Nearly twenty years."

"Was he born in this neighborhood?"

"I think he came from the West."

"Does he say from what part of the western country?"

"He says very little about his past life."

Roland Reed smiled significantly.

"Perhaps he has his reasons," he said meditatively.

"Is he thought to be rich?" he asked, after a pause.

"Yes, but how rich no one knows. He is taxed for his house and grounds, but he may have a good deal of property besides. It is generally thought he has."

"He does not appear to be friendly toward your son."

"No," answered Mrs. Larkin, with a trace of indignation, "though I am sure he has no cause to dislike him. He seemed convinced that Luke had come by your tin box dishonestly."

"It seemed to me that he was prejudiced against Luke. How do you account for it?"

"Perhaps his son, Randolph, has influenced him."

"So he has a son—how old?"

"Almost Luke's age. He thinks Luke beneath him, though why he should do so, except that Luke is poor, I can't understand. Not long since there was a skating match for a prize of a Waterbury watch, offered by the grammar-school teacher, which Luke would have won had not Randolph arranged with another boy to get in his way and leave the victory to him."

"So Randolph won the watch?"

"Yes."

"I suppose he had a watch of his own already."

"Yes, a silver one, while Luke had none. This makes it meaner in him."

"I don't mind it now, mother," said Luke, who had overheard the last part of the conversation. "He is welcome to his watches—I can wait."

"Has Squire Duncan shown his hostility to Luke in any other way?" inquired the stranger.

"Yes; Luke has for over a year been janitor at the schoolhouse. It didn't bring much—only a dollar a week—but it was considerable to us. Lately Squire Duncan was appointed on the school committee to fill a vacancy, and his first act was to remove Luke from his position."

"Not in favor of his son, I conclude."

Luke laughed.

"Randolph would be shocked at the mere supposition," he said. "He is a young man who wears kid gloves, and the duties of a school janitor he would look upon as degrading."

"I really think, Luke, you have been badly treated," said Roland Reed, with a friendly smile.

"I have thought so, too, sir, but I suppose I have no better claim to the office than any other boy."

"You needed the income, however."

"Yes, sir."

By this time they were at the door of the cottage.

"Won't you come in, sir?" asked Mrs. Larkin, cordially.

"Thank you. I will not only do so, but as I don't care to stay at the hotel, I will even crave leave to pass the night under your roof."

"If you don't mind our poor accommodations, you will be very welcome."

"I am not likely to complain, Mrs. Larkin. I have not been nursed in the lap of luxury. For two years I was a California miner, and camped out. For that long period I did not know what it was to sleep in a bed. I used to stretch myself in a blanket, and lie down on the ground."

"You won't have to do that here, Mr. Reed," said Luke, smiling. "But it must have been great fun."

"How can you say so, Luke?" expostulated his mother. "It must have been very uncomfortable, and dangerous to the health."

"I wouldn't mind it a bit, mother," said Luke, stoutly.

Roland Reed smiled.

"I am not surprised that you and your mother regard the matter from different points of view," he said. "It is only natural. Women are not adapted to roughing it. Boys like nothing better, and so with young men. But there comes a time—when a man passes forty—when he sets a higher value on the comforts of life. I don't mind confessing that I wouldn't care to repeat my old mining experiences."

"I hope you were repaid for your trouble and privations, sir."

"Yes, I was handsomely repaid. I may soon be as rich as your local magnate, Prince Duncan, but I have had to work harder for it, probably."

"So you know the squire's name?" said Mrs. Larkin, in some surprise.

"I must have heard it somewhere," remarked Roland Reed. "Have I got it right?"

"Yes; it's a peculiar name."

When they reached the cottage Mrs. Larkin set about getting supper. In honor of her guest she sent out for some steak, and baked some biscuit, so that the table presented an inviting appearance when the three sat down to it. After supper was over, Roland Reed said: "I told you that I wished to speak to you on business, Mrs. Larkin. It is briefly this: Are you willing to receive a boarder?"

"I am afraid, sir, that you would hardly be satisfied with our humble accommodations."

"Oh, I am not speaking of myself, but of a child. I am a widower, Mrs. Larkin, and have a little daughter eight years of age. She is now boarding in New York, but I do not like the people with whom I have placed her. She is rather delicate, also, and I think a country town would suit her better than the city air. I should like to have her under just such nice motherly care as I am sure you would give her."

"I shall be very glad to receive her," said Mrs. Larkin, with a flush of pleasure.

"And for the terms?"

"I would rather you would name them, sir."

"Then I will say ten dollars a week."

"Ten dollars!" exclaimed the widow, in amazement. "It won't be worth half that."

"I don't pay for board merely, but for care and attendance as well. She may be sick, and that would increase your trouble."

"She would in that case receive as much care as if she were my own daughter; but I don't ask such an exorbitant rate of board."

"It isn't exorbitant if I choose to pay it, Mrs. Larkin," said Mr. Reed, smiling. "I am entirely able to pay that price, and prefer to do so."

"It will make me feel quite rich, sir," said the widow, gratefully. "I shall find it useful, especially as Luke has lost his situation."

"Luke may find another position."

"When do you wish your daughter to come?" asked Mrs. Larkin.

"Luke will accompany me to the city to-morrow, and bring her back with him. By the way, I will pay you four weeks in advance."

He drew four ten-dollar bills from his pocket and put them into the widow's hand.

"I am almost afraid this is a dream," said Mrs. Larkin. "You have made me very happy."

"You mustn't become purse-proud, mother," said Luke, "because you have become suddenly rich."

"Can you be ready to take the first train to New York with me in the morning, Luke?" asked Roland Reed.

"Yes, sir; it starts at half-past seven."

"Your breakfast will be ready on time," said the widow, "and Luke will call you."

CHAPTER XVI

LUKE'S VISIT TO NEW YORK

THE morning train to New York carried among its passengers Luke and his new friend. The distance was thirty-five miles, and the time occupied was a trifle over an hour. The two sat together, and Luke had an opportunity of observing his companion more closely. He was a man of middle age, dark complexion, with keen black eyes, and the expression of one who understood the world and was well fitted to make his way in it. He had already given the Larkins to understand that he had been successful in accumulating money.

As for Luke, he felt happy and contented. The tide of fortune seemed to have turned in his favor, or rather in favor of his family. The handsome weekly sum which would be received for the board of Mr. Reed's little daughter would be sufficient of itself to defray the modest expenses of their household. If he, too, could obtain work, they would actually feel rich.

"Luke," said his companion, "does your mother own the cottage where you live?"

"Yes, sir."

"Free of incumbrance?"

"Not quite. There is a mortgage of three hundred dollars held by Squire Duncan. It was held by Deacon Tibbetts, but about three months since Squire Duncan bought it."

"What could be his object in buying it?"

"I don't know, sir. Perhaps the deacon owed him money."

"I am surprised, then, that he deprived you of your position as janitor, since it would naturally make it more difficult for you to meet the interest."

"That is true, sir. I wondered at it myself."

"Your house is a small one, but the location is fine. It would make a building lot suitable for a gentleman's summer residence."

"Yes, sir; there was a gentleman in the village last summer who called upon mother and tried to induce her to sell."

"Did he offer her a fair price?"

"No, sir; he said he should have to take down the cottage, and he only offered eight hundred dollars. Mother would have sold for a thousand."

"Tell her not to accept even that offer, but to hold on to the property. Some day she can obtain considerably more."

"She won't sell unless she is obliged to," replied Luke. "A few days since I thought we might have to do it. Now, with the generous sum which you allow for your little girl's board there will be no necessity."

"Has Squire Duncan broached the subject to your mother?"

"He mentioned it one day, but he wanted her to sell for seven hundred dollars."

"He is evidently sharp at a bargain."

"Yes, sir; he is not considered liberal."

There was one thing that troubled Luke in spite of the pleasure he anticipated from his visit to New York. He knew very well that his clothes were shabby, and he shrank from the idea of appearing on Broadway in a patched suit too small for him. But he had never breathed a word of complaint to his mother, knowing that she could not afford to buy him another suit, and he did not wish to add to her troubles. It might have happened that occasionally he fixed a troubled look on his clothes, but if Roland Reed noticed it he did not make any comment.

But when they reached New York, and found themselves on Broadway, his companion paused in front of a large clothing store with large plate-glass windows, and said, quietly: "Come in, Luke. I think you need some new clothes."

Luke's face flushed with pleasure, but he said, "I have no money, Mr. Reed."

"I have," said Roland Reed, significantly.

"You are very kind, sir," said Luke, gratefully.

"It costs little to be kind when you have more money than you know what to do with," said Reed. "I don't mean that I am a Vanderbilt or an Astor, but my income is much greater than I need to spend on myself."

A suit was readily found which fitted Luke as well as if it had been made for him. It was of gray mixed cloth, made in fashionable style.

"You may as well keep it on, Luke." Then to the shopman: "Have you a nice suit of black cloth, and of the same size?"

"Yes, sir," answered the salesman, readily.

"He may as well have two while we are about it. As to the

old suit, it is too small, and we will leave it here to be given away to some smaller boy."

Luke was quite overwhelmed by his new friend's munificence.

"I don't think mother will know me," he said, as he surveyed himself in a long mirror.

"Then I will introduce you or give you a letter of introduction. Have you a watch, Luke?"

"No, sir; you know I did not get the prize at the skating match."

"True; then I must remedy the deficiency."

They took the roadway stage down below the Astor House—it was before the days of Jacob Sharp's horse railway—and got out at Benedict's. There Mr. Reed made choice of a neat silver watch, manufactured at Waltham, and bought a plated chain to go with it.

"Put that in your vest pocket," he said. "It may console you for the loss of the Waterbury."

"How can I ever repay you for your kindness, Mr. Reed?" said Luke, overjoyed.

"I have taken a fancy to you, Luke," said his companion. "I hope to do more for you soon. Now we will go uptown, and I will put my little girl under your charge."

Luke had dreaded making a call at a nice city house in his old suit. Now he looked forward to it with pleasure, especially after his new friend completed his benefactions by buying him a new pair of shoes and a hat.

"Luke," asked his companion, as they were on their way uptown in a Sixth Avenue car, "do you know who owned the box of bonds taken from the Groveton Bank?"

"I have heard that it was a Mr. Armstrong, now traveling in Europe."

"How did he come to leave the box in a village bank?"

"He is some acquaintance of Squire Duncan, and spent some weeks last summer at the village hotel."

"Then probably he left the box there at the suggestion of Duncan, the president."

"I don't know, sir, but I think it very likely."

"Humph! This is getting interesting. The contents of the box were government bonds, I have heard."

"I heard Squire Duncan say so."

"Were they coupon or registered?"

"What difference would that make, sir?"

"The first could be sold without trouble by the thief, while the last could not be disposed of without a formal transfer from the owner."

"Then it would not pay to steal them?"

"Just so. Luke, do you know, a strange idea has come into my head."

"What is it, sir?"

"I think Prince Duncan knows more about how those bonds were spirited away than is suspected."

Luke was greatly surprised.

"You don't think he took them himself, do you?" he asked.

"That remains to be seen. It is a curious affair altogether. I may have occasion to speak of it another time. Are you a good writer?"

"Fair, I believe, sir."

"I have recently come into possession of a business in a city in Ohio, which I carry on through a paid agent. Among other things, I have bought out the old accounts. I shall need to have a large number of bills made out, covering a series of years, which I shall then put into the hands of a collector and realize so far as I can. This work, with a little instruction, I think you can do."

"I shall be very glad to do it, sir."

"You will be paid fairly for the labor."

"I don't need any pay, Mr. Reed. You have already paid me handsomely."

"You refer to the clothing and the watch? Those are gifts. I will pay you thirty cents an hour for the time employed, leaving you to keep the account. The books of the firm I have at the house where my daughter is boarding. You will take them back to Groveton with you."

"This is a fortunate day for me," said Luke. "It will pay me much better than the janitorship."

"Do your duty, Luke, and your good fortune will continue. But here is our street."

They left the car at the corner of Fourteenth Street and Sixth Avenue, and turning westward, paused in front of a four-story house of good appearance.

CHAPTER XVII

RANDOLPH IS MYSTIFIED

IN AN hour, Luke, with the little girl under his charge, was on his way to the depot, accompanied by Mr. Reed, who paid for their tickets, and bade them good-bye, promising to communicate with Luke.

Rosa Reed was a bright little girl of about eight years of age. She made no opposition to going with Luke, but put her hand confidently in his, and expressed much pleasure at the prospect of living in the country. She had been under the care of two maiden ladies, the Misses Graham, who had no love for children, and had merely accepted the charge on account of the liberal terms paid them by the father. They seemed displeased at the withdrawal of Rosa, and clearly signified this by their cold, stiff reception of Mr. Reed and Luke.

"The old girls don't like to part with Rosa," he said, with a smile, as they emerged into the street.

"Are you sorry to leave them, Rosa?" he inquired.

"No; they ain't a bit pleasant," answered the little girl, decidedly.

"Were they strict with you?" asked Luke.

"Yes; they were always saying, 'Little girls should be seen and not heard!' They didn't want me to make a bit of noise, and wouldn't let me have any little girls in to play with me. Are there any little girls at your home?"

"No, but there are some living near by, and they will come to see you."

"That will be nice," said Rosa, with satisfaction.

Directions were left to have the little girl's trunk go to Groveton by express, and, therefore, Luke was encumbered only by a small satchel belonging to his new charge.

Of the details of the journey it is unnecessary to speak. The two young travelers arrived at Groveton, and, as it chanced, reached Luke's cottage without attracting much observation. The door was opened by the widow, whose kind manner at once won the favor of the child.

"I like you much better than Miss Graham," she said, with childish frankness.

"I am glad of that, my child," said Mrs. Larkin. "I will try to make this a pleasant home for you."

"I like Luke, too," said Rosa.

"Really, Rosa, you make me blush," said Luke. "I am not used to hearing young ladies say they like me."

"I think he is a good boy," said Rosa, reflectively. "Isn't he, Mrs. Larkin?"

"I think so, my dear," said the widow, smiling.

"Then I suppose I shall have to behave like one," said Luke. "Do you think I have improved in appearance, mother?"

"I noticed your new suit at once, Luke."

"I have another in this bundle, mother; and that isn't all. Do you see this watch? I sha'n't mourn the loss of the Waterbury any longer."

"Mr. Reed is certainly proving a kind friend, Luke. We have much reason to be grateful."

"He has also provided me with employment for a time, mother." And then Luke told his mother about the copying he had engaged to do.

It is hardly necessary to say that the heart of the widow was unfeignedly thankful for the favorable change in their fortunes, and she did not omit to give thanks to Providence for raising up so kind and serviceable a friend.

About the middle of the afternoon Luke made his appearance in the village street. Though I hope my readers will not suspect him of being a dude, he certainly did enjoy the consciousness of being well dressed. He hoped he should meet Randolph, anticipating the surprise and disappointment of the latter at the evidence of his prosperity.

When Luke was arrested, Randolph rejoiced as only a mean and spiteful boy would be capable of doing at the humiliation and anticipated disgrace of a boy whom he disliked. He had indulged in more than one expression of triumph, and sought every opportunity of discussing the subject, to the disgust of all fair-minded persons. Even Sam Noble protested, though a toady of Randolph.

"Look here, Randolph," he said, "I don't like Luke overmuch, and I know he doesn't like me, but I don't believe he's a thief, and I am sorry he is in trouble."

"Then you are no friend of mine," said Randolph, looking black.

"Oh, I say, Randolph, you know better than that. Haven't I always stood up for you, and done whatever you wanted me to?"

"If you were my friend you wouldn't stand up for Luke."

"I am not a friend of his, and I am a friend of yours, but I don't want him to go to prison."

"I do, if he deserves it."

"I don't believe he does deserve it."

"That is what I complain of in you."

"The fact is, Randolph, you expect too much. If you want to break friendship, all right."

Randolph was amazed at this unexpected independence on the part of one whom he regarded as his bond slave; but, being hardly prepared to part with him, especially as his other follower, Tom Harper, had partially thrown off his allegiance, thought it prudent to be satisfied with Sam's expressions of loyalty, even if they did not go as far as he wished.

Randolph missed Luke at school on the day after the trial. Of course, he had no idea that our hero was out of school, and hastily concluded that on account of his trial he was ashamed to show himself.

"I don't wonder he doesn't want to show himself," he remarked to Tom Harper.

"Why not? He has been acquitted."

"Never mind. He has been under arrest, and may yet be guilty in spite of his acquittal. Have you seen him to-day?"

"No."

"Probably he is hiding at home. Well, it shows some sort of shame."

On his way home from school Randolph was destined to be surprised. Not far from his own house he met Luke, arrayed in his new suit, with a chain that looked like gold crossing his waistcoat. Instead of looking confused and ashamed, Luke looked uncommonly bright and cheerful.

Randolph was amazed. What could it all mean? He had intended not to notice Luke, but to pass him with a scornful smile, but his curiosity got the better of him.

"Why were you not at school to-day?" he asked, abruptly.

Luke smiled.

"I didn't think you would miss me, Randolph."

"I didn't, but wondered at your absence."

"I was detained by business. I expect to have the pleasure of seeing you there to-morrow."

"Humph! You seem to have invested in a new suit."

"Yes; my old suit was getting decidedly shabby, as you kindly remarked at Florence Grant's party."

"Where did you get them?"

"In New York."

"In New York!" repeated Randolph, in surprise. "When did you go there?"

"This morning. It was that which detained me from school."

"I see you've got a new watch-chain, too."

Randolph emphasized the word "chain" satirically, being under the impression that no watch was attached.

"Yes; you may like to see my new watch." And Luke, with pardonable triumph, produced his new watch, which was a stem-winder, whereas Randolph's was only a key-winder.

Randolph condescended to take the watch in his hands and examine it.

"Where was this bought?" he asked.

"At Benedict's."

"You seem to have plenty of money," he said, with unpleasant significance.

"I should like more."

"Only you are rather imprudent in making such extensive purchases so soon after your trial."

"What do you mean?" demanded Luke quickly.

"What should I mean? It is evident that you robbed the bank, after all. I shall tell my father, and you may find your trouble is not over."

"Look here, Randolph Duncan!" said Luke sternly, "I look upon that as an insult, and I don't mean to be insulted. I am no more a thief than you are, and that you know."

"Do you mean to charge me with being a thief?" fumed Randolph.

"No; I only say you are as much a thief as I am. If you repeat your insult, I shall be obliged to knock you down."

"You impudent loafer!" screamed Randolph. "You'll be sorry for this. I'll have you arrested over again."

"I have no doubt you would if you had the power. I sha'n't lie awake nights thinking of it. If you have nothing more to say I will leave you."

Randolph did not reply, probably because he was at a loss

what to say, but went home angry and mystified. Where could Luke have got his watch and new suit? He asked himself this many times, but no possible explanation suggested itself.

Scarcely had Luke parted with Randolph when he met his friend Linton, who surveyed Luke's improved appearance with pleasure and surprise.

"I say, Luke, are you setting up for a dude?"

"I thought a little of it," answered Luke, with a smile—and then he explained the cause of his good fortune. "I have only one regret," he added, "Randolph seems to be grieved over it. He liked me better in my old suit. Besides, I have a new watch, and it turns out to be better than his."

Here he displayed his new silver watch. Linton felt a generous pleasure in Luke's luck, and it may truly be said rejoiced more at it than he would at any piece of good fortune to himself.

"By the way, Luke," he said, "I am going to give a party next Thursday evening, and I give you the very first invitation. It is my birthday, you know."

"I accept with pleasure, sir. I look upon you as my warmest friend, and as long as I retain your friendship I shall not care for Randolph's malice."

CHAPTER XVIII

MR. DUNCAN'S SECRET

ABOUT two weeks later, Prince Duncan sat at his desk with a troubled look. Open before him were letters. One was postmarked London, and ran as follows:

"MY DEAR SIR: I have decided to shorten my visit, and shall leave Liverpool next Saturday en route for New York. You will see, therefore, that I shall arrive nearly as soon as the letter I am now writing. I have decided to withdraw the box of securities I deposited in your bank, and shall place it in a safe-deposit vault in New York. You may expect to see me shortly.

"Yours in haste,

"JOHN ARMSTRONG."

Drops of perspiration gathered on the brow of Prince Duncan as he read this letter. What would Mr. Armstrong say when he learned that the box had mysteriously disappeared? That he would be thoroughly indignant, and make it very unpleasant for the president of Groveton Bank, was certain. He would ask, among other things, why Mr. Duncan had not informed him of the loss by cable, and no satisfactory explanation could be given. He would ask, furthermore, why detectives had not been employed to ferret out the mystery, and here again no satisfactory explanation could be given. Prince Duncan knew very well that he had a reason, but it was not one that could be disclosed.

He next read the second letter, and his trouble was not diminished. It was from a Wall Street broker, informing him that the Erie shares bought for him on a margin had gone down two points, and it would be necessary for him to deposit additional margin, or be sold out.

"Why did I ever invest in Erie?" thought Duncan ruefully. "I was confidently assured that it would go up—that it must go up—and here it is falling, and Heaven knows how much lower it will go."

At this point the door opened, and Randolph entered. He had a special favor to ask. He had already given his father several hints that he would like a gold watch, being quite dissatisfied with his silver watch now that Luke Larkin possessed one superior to his. He had chosen a very unfavorable moment for his request, as he soon found out.

"Father," he said, "I have a favor to ask."

"What is it?" asked Prince Duncan, with a frown.

"I wish you would buy me a gold watch."

"Oh, you do!" sneered his father. "I was under the impression that you had two watches already."

"So I have, but one is a Waterbury, and the other a cheap silver one."

"Well, they keep time, don't they?"

"Yes."

"Then what more do you want?"

"Luke Larkin has a silver watch better than mine—a stem-winder."

"Suppose he has?"

"I don't want a working boy like him to outshine me."

"Where did he get his watch?"

"I don't know; he won't tell. Will you buy me a gold one, father? Then I can look down upon him again."

"No, I can't. Money is very scarce with me just now."

"Then I don't want to wear a watch at all," said Randolph pettishly.

"Suit yourself," said his father coldly. "Now you may leave the room. I am busy."

Randolph left the room. He would have slammed the door behind him, but he knew his father's temper, and he did not dare to do so.

"What am I to do?" Prince Duncan asked himself anxiously. "I must send money to the brokers, or they will sell me out, and I shall meet with a heavy loss."

After a little thought he wrote a letter enclosing a check, but dated it two days ahead.

"They will think it a mistake," he thought, "and it will give me time to turn around. Now for money to meet the check when it arrives."

Prince Duncan went up-stairs, and, locking the door of his chamber, opened a large trunk in one corner of the room. From under a pile of clothing he took out a tin box, and with hands that trembled with excitement he extracted therefrom a dozen government bonds. One was for ten thousand dollars, one for five, and the remainder were for one thousand dollars each.

"If they were only sold, and the money deposited in the bank to my credit," he thought. "I am almost sorry I started in this thing. The risk is very great, but—but I must have money."

At this moment some one tried the door.

Prince Duncan turned pale, and the bonds nearly fell from his hands.

"Who's there?" he asked.

"It is I, papa," answered Randolph.

"Then you may go down-stairs again," answered his father angrily. "I don't want to be disturbed."

"Won't you open the door a minute? I just want to ask a question."

"No, I won't. Clear out!" exclaimed the bank president angrily.

"What a frightful temper father has!" thought the discomfited Randolph.

There was nothing for it but to go down-stairs, and he did so in a very discontented frame of mind.

"It seems to me that something is going contrary," said Duncan to himself. "It is clear that it won't do to keep these bonds here any longer. I must take them to New York to-morrow—and raise money on them."

On second thought, to-morrow he decided only to take the five-thousand-dollar bond, and five of the one thousand, fearing that too large a sale at one time might excite suspicion.

Carefully selecting the bonds referred to, he put them away in a capacious pocket, and, locking the trunk, went down-stairs again.

"There is still time to take the eleven-o'clock train," he said, consulting his watch. "I must do it."

Seeking his wife, he informed her that he would take the next train for New York.

"Isn't this rather sudden?" she asked, in surprise.

"A little, perhaps, but I have a small matter of business to attend to. Besides, I think the trip will do me good. I am not feeling quite as well as usual."

"I believe I will go, too," said Mrs. Duncan unexpectedly. "I want to make some purchases at Stewart's."

This suggestion was very far from agreeable to her husband.

"Really—I am"—he said, "I must disappoint you. My time will be wholly taken up by matters of business, and I can't go with you."

"You don't need to. I can take care of myself, and we can meet at the depot at four o'clock."

"Besides, I can't supply you with any money for shopping."

'I have enough. I might have liked a little more, but I can make it do."

"Perhaps it will look better if we go in company," thought Prince Duncan. "She needn't be in my way, for we can part at the station."

"Very well, Jane," he said quietly. "If you won't expect me to dance attendance upon you, I withdraw my objections."

The eleven-o'clock train for New York had among its passengers Mr. and Mrs. Duncan.

There was another passenger whom neither of them noticed—a small, insignificant-looking man—who occasionally directed a quick glance at the portly bank president.

CHAPTER XIX

EFFECTING A LOAN

PRINCE DUNCAN was unusually taciturn during the railroad journey—so much so that his wife noticed it, and inquired the reason.

"Business, my dear," answered the bank president. "I am rather perplexed by a matter of business."

"Business connected with the bank, Mr. Duncan?" asked his wife.

"No, private business."

"Have you heard anything yet of the stolen bonds?"

"Not yet."

"Have you any suspicion?"

"None that I am at liberty to mention," answered Duncan, looking mysterious.

"I suppose you no longer suspect that boy Luke?"

"I don't know. The man who owns to having given him the tin box for safe-keeping is, in my opinion, a suspicious character. I shouldn't be at all surprised if he were a jailbird."

The small man already referred to, who occupied a seat just across the aisle, here smiled slightly, but whether at the president's remark, is not clear.

"What did he call himself?"

"Roland Reed—no doubt an alias."

"It seems to me you ought to follow him up, and see if you can't convict him of the theft."

"You may be sure, Jane, that the president and directors of the Groveton Bank will do their duty in this matter," said Mr. Duncan rather grandiloquently. "By the way, I have received this morning a letter from Mr. Armstrong, the owner of the stolen bonds, saying that he will be at home in a few days."

"Does he know of the loss?"

"Not yet."

"How will he take it?"

"Really, Jane, you are very inquisitive this morning. I presume he will be very much annoyed."

The car had become quite warm, and Mr. Duncan, who had

hitherto kept on his overcoat, rose to take it off. Unfortunately for him he quite forgot the bonds he had in the inside pocket, and in his careless handling of the coat the package fell upon the floor of the car, one slipping out of the envelope—a bond for one thousand dollars.

Prince Duncan turned pale, and stooped to pick up the package. But the small man opposite was too quick for him. He raised the package from the floor, and handing it to the bank president with a polite bow, said, with a smile: "You wouldn't like to lose this, sir."

"No," answered Duncan gruffly, angry with the other for anticipating him, "it was awkward of me."

Mrs. Duncan also saw the bond, and inquired with natural curiosity: "Do they belong to the bank, Mr. Duncan?"

"No; they are my own."

"I am glad of that. What are you going to do with them?"

"Hush! It is dangerous to speak of them here. Some one might hear, and I might be followed. I am very much annoyed that they have been seen at all."

This closed Mrs. Duncan's mouth, but she resolved to make further inquiries when they were by themselves.

Prince Duncan looked askance at his opposite neighbor. He was a man who had come to Groveton recently, and had opened a billiard saloon and bar not far from the bank. He was not regarded as a very desirable citizen, and had already excited the anxiety of parents by luring into the saloon some of the boys and young men of the village. Among them, though Squire Duncan did not know it, was his own son Randolph, who had already developed quite a fondness for playing pool, and even occasionally patronized the bar. This, had he known it, would have explained Randolph's increased applications for money.

Whether Tony Denton—his full name was Anthony Denton—had any special object in visiting New York, I am unable to state. At all events it appeared that his business lay in the same direction as that of Prince Duncan, for on the arrival of the train at the New York depot, he followed the bank president at a safe distance, and was clearly bent upon keeping him in view.

Mr. Duncan walked slowly, and appeared to be plunged in anxious thought. His difficulties were by no means over. He had the bonds to dispose of, and he feared the large amount might occasion suspicion. They were coupon bonds, and bore no name or other evidence of ownership. Yet the mere fact of having such a large amount might occasion awkward inquiries.

"Here's yer mornin' papers!" called a negro newsboy, thrusting his bundle in front of the country banker.

"Give me a *Herald*," said Mr. Duncan. Opening the paper, his eye ran hastily over the columns. It lighted up as he saw a particular advertisement.

"The very thing," he said to himself.

This was the advertisement:

"LOAN OFFICE—We are prepared to loan sums to suit, on first-class security, at a fair rate of interest. Call or address Sharp & Ketchum, No. — Wall Street. Third floor."

"I will go there," Prince Duncan suddenly decided. "I will borrow what I can on these bonds, and being merely held on collateral, they will be kept out of the market. At the end of six months, say, I will redeem them, or order them sold, and collect the balance, minus the interest."

Having arrived at this conclusion, he quickened his pace, his expression became more cheerful, and he turned his steps toward Wall Street.

"What did the old fellow see in the paper?" thought Tony Denton, who, still undiscovered, followed Mr. Duncan closely. "It is something that pleased him, evidently."

He beckoned the same newsboy, bought a *Herald* also, and turning to that part of the paper on which the banker's eyes had been resting, discovered Sharp & Ketchum's advertisement.

"That's it, I'll bet a hat," he decided. "He is going to raise money on the bonds. I'll follow him."

When Duncan turned into Wall Street, Tony Denton felt that he had guessed correctly. He was convinced when the bank president paused before the number indicated in the advertisement.

"It won't do for me to follow him in," he said to himself, "nor will it be necessary—I can remember the place and turn it to my own account by and by."

Prince Duncan went up-stairs, and paused before a door on which was inscribed:

SHARP & KETCHUM
BANKERS
LOANS NEGOTIATED

He opened the door, and found the room furnished in the style of a private banking-office.

"Is Mr. Sharp or Mr. Ketchum in?" he inquired of a sharp-faced young clerk, the son, as it turned out, of the senior partner.

"Yes, sir, Mr. Sharp is in."

"Is he at leisure? I wish to see him on business."

"Go in there, sir," said the clerk, pointing to a small private room in the corner of the office. Following the directions, Mr. Duncan found himself in the presence of a man of about fifty, with a hatchet face, much puckered with wrinkles, and a very foxy expression.

"I am Mr. Sharp," he said, in answer to an inquiry.

Prince Duncan unfolded his business. He wished to borrow eight or nine thousand dollars on ten thousand dollars' worth of United States Government bonds.

"Why don't you sell at once?" asked Sharp keenly.

"Because I wish, for special reasons, to redeem these identical bonds, say six months hence."

"They are your own?" asked Mr. Sharp.

"They are a part of my wife's estate, of which I have control. I do not, however, wish her to know that I have raised money on them," answered Duncan, with a smooth falsehood.

"Of course, that makes a difference. However, I will loan you seven thousand dollars, and you will give me your note for seven thousand five hundred, at the usual interest, with permission to sell the bonds at the end of six months if the note remains unpaid then, I to hand you the balance."

Prince Duncan protested against these terms as exorbitant, but was finally obliged to accede to them. On the whole, he was fairly satisfied. The check would relieve him from all his embarrassments and give him a large surplus.

"So far so good!" said Tony Denton, as he saw Mr. Duncan emerge into the street. "If I am not greatly mistaken this will prove a lucky morning for me."

CHAPTER XX

LUKE TALKS WITH A CAPITALIST

LUKE worked steadily on the task given him by his new patron. During the first week he averaged three hours a day, with an additional two hours on Saturday, making, in all, twenty hours, making, at thirty cents per hour, six dollars. This Luke considered fair pay, considering that he was attending school and maintaining good rank in his classes.

"Why don't we see more of you, Luke?" asked his friend Linton one day. "You seem to stay in the house all the time."

"Because I am at work, Linny. Last week I made six dollars."

"How?" asked Linton, surprised.

"By copying and making out bills for Mr. Reed."

"That is better than being janitor at a dollar a week."

"Yes, but I have to work a good deal harder."

"I am afraid you are working too hard."

"I shouldn't like to keep it up, but it is only for a short time. If I gave up school I should find it easy enough, but I don't want to do that."

"No, I hope you won't; I should miss you, and so would all the boys."

"Including Randolph Duncan?"

"I don't know about that. By the way, I hear that Randolph is spending a good deal of his time at Tony Denton's billiard saloon."

"I am sorry to hear it. It hasn't a very good reputation."

One day Luke happened to be at the depot at the time of the arrival of the train from New York. A small, elderly man stepped upon the platform whom Luke immediately recognized as John Armstrong, the owner of the missing box of bonds. He was surprised to see him, having supposed that he was still in Europe. Mr. Armstrong, as already stated, had boarded for several weeks during the preceding summer at Groveton.

He looked at Luke with a half-glance of recognition.

"Haven't I seen you before?" he said. "What is your name?"

"My name is Luke Larkin. I saw you several times last summer."

"Then you know me?"

"Yes, sir, you are Mr. Armstrong. But I thought you were in Europe."

"So I was till recently. I came home sooner than I expected."

Luke was not surprised. He supposed that intelligence of the robbery had hastened Mr. Armstrong's return.

"I suppose it was the news of your box that hurried you home," Luke ventured to say.

"No, I hadn't heard of it till my arrival in New York. Can you tell me anything about the matter? Has the box been found?"

"Not that I have heard, sir."

"Was, or is, anybody suspected?"

"I was suspected," answered Luke, smiling, "but I don't think any one suspects me now."

"You!" exclaimed the capitalist, in evident astonishment. "What could induce any one to suspect a boy like you of robbing a bank?"

"There was some ground for it," said Luke candidly. "A tin box, of the same appearance as the one lost, was seen in our house. I was arrested on suspicion, and tried."

"You don't say so! How did you prove your innocence?"

"The gentleman who gave me the box in charge appeared and testified in my favor. But for that I am afraid I should have fared badly."

"That is curious. Who was the gentleman?"

Luke gave a rapid history of the circumstances already known to the reader.

"I am glad to hear this, being principally interested in the matter. However, I never should have suspected you. I claim to be something of a judge of character and physiognomy, and your appearance is in your favor. Your mother is a widow, I believe?"

"Yes, sir."

"And you are the janitor of the schoolhouse?"

Mr. Armstrong was a close observer, and though having large interests of his own, made himself familiar with the affairs of those whom others in his position would wholly have ignored.

"I was janitor," Luke replied, "but when Mr. Duncan became a member of the school committee he removed me."

"For what reason?" asked Mr. Armstrong quickly.

"I don't think he ever liked me, and his son Randolph and I have never been good friends."

"You mean Mr. Duncan, the president of the bank?"

"Yes, sir?"

"Why are not you and his son friends?"

"I don't know, sir. He has always been in the habit of sneering at me as a poor boy—a working boy—and unworthy to associate with him."

"You don't look like a poor boy. You are better dressed than I was at your age. Besides, you have a watch, I judge from the chain."

"Yes, sir; but all that is only lately. I have found a good friend who has been very kind to me."

"Who is he?"

"Roland Reed, the owner of the tin box I referred to."

"Roland Reed! I never heard the name. Where is he from?"

"From the West, I believe, though at present he is staying in New York."

"How much were you paid as janitor?"

"A dollar a week."

"That is very little. Is the amount important to you?"

"No, sir, not now." And then Luke gave particulars of the good fortune of the family in having secured a profitable boarder, and, furthermore, in obtaining for himself profitable employment.

"This Mr. Reed seems to be a kind-hearted and liberal man. I am glad for your sake. I sympathize with poor boys. Can you guess the reason?"

"Were you a poor boy yourself, sir?"

"I was, and a very poor boy. When I was a boy of thirteen and fourteen I ran around in overalls and bare-footed. But I don't think it did me any harm," the old man added, musingly. "It kept me from squandering money on foolish pleasures, for I had none to spend; it made me industrious and self-reliant, and when I obtained employment it made me anxious to please my employer."

"I hope it will have the same effect on me, sir."

"I hope so, and I think so. What sort of a boy is this son of Mr. Duncan?"

"If his father were not a rich man, I think he would be more agreeable. As it is, he seems to have a high idea of his own importance."

"So his father has the reputation of being a rich man, eh?"

"Yes, sir. We have always considered him so."

"Without knowing much about it?"

"Yes, sir; we judged from his style of living, and from his being president of a bank."

"That amounts to nothing. His salary as president is only moderate."

"I am sorry you should have met with such a loss, Mr. Armstrong."

"So am I, but it won't cripple me. Still, a man doesn't like to lose twenty-five thousand dollars and over."

"Was there as much as that in the box, sir?" asked Luke, in surprise.

"Yes, I don't know why I need make any secret of it. There were twenty-five thousand dollars in government bonds, and these, at present rates, are worth in the neighborhood of thirty thousand dollars."

"That seems to me a great deal of money," said Luke.

"It is, but I can spare it without any diminution of comfort. I don't feel, however, like pocketing the loss without making a strong effort to recover the money. I didn't expect to meet immediately upon arrival the only person hitherto suspected of accomplishing the robbery."

He smiled as he spoke, and Luke saw that, so far as Mr. Armstrong was concerned, he had no occasion to feel himself under suspicion.

"Are you intending to remain long in Groveton, Mr. Armstrong?" he asked.

"I can't say. I have to see Mr. Duncan about the tin box, and concoct some schemes looking to the discovery of the person or persons concerned in its theft. Have there been any suspicious persons in the village during the last few weeks?"

"Not that I know of, sir."

"What is the character of the men employed in the bank, the cashier and teller?"

"They seem to be very steady young men, sir. I don't think they have been suspected."

"The most dangerous enemies are those who are inside, for they have exceptional opportunities for wrongdoing. Moreover, they have the best chance to cover up their tracks."

"I don't think there is anything to charge against Mr. Roper and Mr. Barclay. They are both young married men, and live in a quiet way."

"Never speculate in Wall Street, eh? One of the soberest,

steadiest bank cashiers I ever knew, who lived plainly and frugally, and was considered by all to be a model man, wrecked the man he was connected with—a small country banker—and is now serving a term in State's prison. The cause was Wall Street speculation. This is more dangerous even than extravagant habits of living."

A part of this conversation took place on the platform of the railroad-station, and a part while they were walking in the direction of the hotel. They had now reached the village inn, and, bidding our hero good morning, Mr. Armstrong entered, and registered his name.

Ten minutes later he set out for the house of Prince Duncan.

CHAPTER XXI

THE DREADED INTERVIEW

MR. DUNCAN had been dreading the inevitable interview with Mr. Armstrong. He knew him to be a sharp man of business, clear-sighted and keen, and he felt that this part of the conference would be an awkward and embarrassing one. He had tried to nerve himself for the interview, and thought he had succeeded, but when the servant brought Mr. Armstrong's card he felt a sinking at his heart, and it was in a tone that betrayed nervousness that he said: "Bring the gentleman in."

"My dear sir," he said, extending his hand and vigorously shaking the hand of his new arrival, "this is an unexpected pleasure."

"Unexpected? Didn't you get my letter from London?" said Mr. Armstrong, suffering his hand to be shaken, but not returning the arm pressure.

"Certainly——"

"In which I mentioned my approaching departure?"

"Yes, certainly; but I didn't know on what day to expect you. Pray sit down. It seems pleasant to see you home safe and well."

"Humph!" returned Armstrong, in a tone by no means as cordial. "Have you found my box of bonds?"

"Not yet, but——"

"Permit me to ask you why you allowed me to remain ignorant

of so important a matter? I was indebted to the public prints, to which my attention was directed by an acquaintance, for a piece of news which should have been communicated to me at once."

"My dear sir, I intended to write you as soon as I heard of your arrival. I did not know till this moment that you were in America."

"You might have inferred it from the intimation in my last letter. Why did you not cable me the news?"

"Because," replied Duncan awkwardly, "I did not wish to spoil your pleasure, and thought from day to day that the box would turn up."

"You were very sparing of my feelings," said Armstrong, dryly—"too much so. I am not a child or an old woman, and it was your imperative duty, in a matter so nearly affecting my interests, to apprise me at once."

"I may have erred in judgment," said Duncan meekly, "but I beg you to believe that I acted as I supposed for the best."

"Leaving that out of consideration at present, let me know what steps you have taken to find out how the box was spirited away, or who was concerned in the robbery."

"I think that you will admit that I acted promptly," said the bank president complacently, "when I say that within twenty-four hours I arrested a party on suspicion of being implicated in the robbery, and tried him myself."

"Who was the party?" asked the capitalist, not betraying the knowledge he had already possessed on the subject.

"A boy in the village named Luke Larkin."

"Humph! What led you to think a boy had broken into the bank? That does not strike me as very sharp on your part."

"I had positive evidence that the boy in question had a tin box concealed in his house—in his mother's trunk. His poverty made it impossible that the box could be his, and I accordingly had him arrested."

"Well, what was the result of the trial?"

"I was obliged to let him go, though by no means satisfied of his innocence."

"Why?"

"A man—a stranger—a very suspicious-looking person, presented himself, and swore that the box was his, and that he had committed it to the charge of this boy."

"Well, that seems tolerably satisfactory, doesn't it?—that is, if he furnished evidence confirming his statement. Did he open the box in court?"

"Yes."

"And the bonds were not there?"

"The bonds were not there—only some papers, and what appeared to be certificates of stock."

"Yet you say you are still suspicious of this man and boy."

"Yes."

"Explain your grounds."

"I thought," replied the president, rather meekly, "he might have taken the bonds from the box and put in other papers."

"That was not very probable. Moreover, he would hardly be likely to leave the box in the village in the charge of a boy."

"The boy might have been his confederate."

"What is the boy's reputation in the village? Has he ever been detected in any act of dishonesty?"

"Not that I know of, but there is one suspicious circumstance to which I would like to call your attention."

"Well?"

"Since this happened Luke has come out in new clothes, and wears a silver watch. The family is very poor, and he could not have had money to buy them unless he obtained some outside aid."

"What, then, do you infer?"

"That he has been handsomely paid for his complicity in the robbery."

"What explanation does he personally give of this unusual expenditure?"

"He admits that they were paid for by this suspicious stranger."

"Has the stranger—what is his name, by the way?"

"Roland Reed, he calls himself, but this, probably, is not his real name."

"Well, has this Reed made his appearance in the village since?"

"If so, he has come during the night, and has not been seen by any of us."

"I can't say I share your suspicion against Mr. Reed. Your theory that he took out the bonds and substituted other papers is far-fetched and improbable. As to the boy, I consider him honest and reliable."

"Do you know Luke Larkin?" asked Mr. Duncan quickly.

"Last summer I observed him somewhat, and never saw anything wrong in him."

"Appearances are deceitful," said the bank president sententiously.

"So I have heard," returned Mr. Armstrong dryly. "But let us go on. What other steps have you taken to discover the lost box?"

"I have had the bank vaults thoroughly searched," answered Duncan, trying to make the best of a weak situation.

"Of course. It is hardly to be supposed that it has been mislaid. Even if it had been it would have turned up before this. Did you discover any traces of the bank being forcibly entered?"

"No; but the burglar may have covered his tracks."

"There would have been something to show an entrance. What is the character of the cashier and teller."

"I know nothing to their disadvantage."

"Then neither have fallen under suspicion?"

"Not as yet," answered the president pointedly.

"It is evident," thought John Armstrong, "that Mr. Duncan is interested in diverting suspicion from some quarter. He is willing that these men should incur suspicion, though it is clear he has none in his own mind."

"Well, what else have you done? Have you employed detectives?" asked Armstrong, impatiently.

"I was about to do so," answered Mr. Duncan, in some embarrassment, "when I heard that you were coming home, and I though I would defer that matter for your consideration."

"Giving time in the meanwhile for the thief or thieves to dispose of their booty? This is very strange conduct, Mr. Duncan."

"I acted for the best," said Prince Duncan.

"You have singular ideas of what is best, then," observed Mr. Armstrong coldly. "It may be too late to remedy your singular neglect, but I will now take the matter out of your hands, and see what I can do."

"Will you employ detectives?" asked Duncan, with evident uneasiness.

Armstrong eyed him sharply, and with growing suspicion.

"I can't say what I will do."

"Have you the numbers of the missing bonds?" asked Duncan anxiously.

"I am not sure. I am afraid I have not."

Was it imagination, or did the bank president look relieved at this statement? John Armstrong made a mental note of this.

After eliciting the particulars of the disappearance of the bonds, John Armstrong rose to go. He intended to return to the city, but he made up his mind to see Luke first. He wanted to inquire the address of Roland Reed.

CHAPTER XXII

LUKE SECURES A NEW FRIEND

LUKE was engaged in copying when Mr. Armstrong called. Though he felt surprised to see his visitor, Luke did not exhibit it in his manner, but welcomed him politely, and invited him into the sitting-room.

"I have called to inquire the address of your friend, Mr. Roland Reed," said Mr. Armstrong. Then, seeing a little uneasiness in Luke's face, he added quickly: "Don't think I have the slightest suspicion of him as regards the loss of the bonds. I wish only to consult him, being myself at a loss what steps to take. He may be able to help me."

Of course, Luke cheerfully complied with his request.

"Has anything been heard yet at the bank?" he asked.

"Nothing whatever. In fact, it does not appear to me that any very serious efforts have been made to trace the robber or robbers. I am left to undertake the task myself."

"If there is anything I can do to help you, Mr. Armstrong, I shall be very glad to do so," said Luke.

"I will bear that in mind, and may call upon you. As yet, my plans are not arranged. Perhaps Mr. Reed, whom I take to be an experienced man of the world, may be able to offer a suggestion. You seem to be at work," he added, with a look at the table at which Luke had been sitting.

"Yes, sir, I am making out some bills for Mr. Reed."

"Is the work likely to occupy you long?"

"No, sir; I shall probably finish the work this week."

"And then your time will be at your disposal?"

"Yes, sir."

"Pardon me the question, but I take it your means are limited?"

"Yes, sir; till recently they have been very limited—now, thanks to Mr. Reed, who pays a liberal salary for his little girl's board, we are very comfortable, and can get along very well, even if I do not immediately find work."

"I am glad to hear that. If I should hear of any employment likely to please you I will send you word."

"Thank you, sir."

"Would you object to leave home?"

"No, sir; there is little or no prospect in Groveton, and though my mother would miss me, she now has company, and I should feel easier about leaving her."

"If you can spare the time, won't you walk with me to the depot?"

"With great pleasure, sir," and Luke went into the adjoining room to fetch his hat, at the same time apprising his mother that he was going out.

On the way to the depot Mr. Armstrong managed to draw out Luke with a view to getting better acquainted with him, and forming an idea of his traits of character. Luke was quite aware of this, but talked frankly and easily, having nothing to conceal.

"A thoroughly good boy, and a smart boy, too!" said Armstrong to himself. "I must see if I can't give him a chance to rise. He seems absolutely reliable."

On the way to the depot they met Randolph Duncan, who eyed them curiously. He recognized Mr. Armstrong as the owner of the stolen bonds—and was a good deal surprised to see him in such friendly conversation with Luke. Knowing Mr. Armstrong to be a rich man, he determined to claim acquaintance.

"How do you do, Mr. Armstrong?" he said, advancing with an ingratiating smile.

"This is Randolph Duncan," said Luke—whom, by the way, Randolph had not thought it necessary to notice.

"I believe I have met the young gentleman before," said Mr. Armstrong politely, but not cordially.

"Yes, sir, I have seen you at our house," continued Randolph—"my father is president of the Groveton Bank. He will be very glad to see you. Won't you come home with me?"

"I have already called upon your father," said Mr. Armstrong.

"I am very sorry your bonds were stolen, Mr. Armstrong."

"Not more than I am, I assure you," returned Mr. Armstrong, with a quizzical smile.

"Could I speak with you a moment in private, sir?" asked Randolph, with a significant glance at Luke.

"Certainly; Luke, will you cross the road a minute? Now, young man!"

"Probably you don't know that the boy you are walking with was suspected of taking the box from the bank."

"I have heard so; but he was acquitted of the charge, wasn't he?"

"My father still believes that he had something to do with it, and so do I," added Randolph, with an emphatic nod of his head.

"Isn't he a friend of yours?" asked Mr. Armstrong quietly.

"No, indeed; we go to the same school, though father thinks of sending me to an academy out of town soon, but there is no friendship between us. He is only a working boy."

"Humph! That is very much against him," observed Mr. Armstrong, but it was hard to tell from his tone whether he spoke in earnest or ironically.

"Oh, well, he has to work, for the family is very poor. He's come out in new clothes and a silver watch since the robbery. He says the strange man from whom he received a tin box just like yours gave them to him."

"And you think he didn't get them in that way?"

"Yes, I think they were leagued together. I feel sure that man robbed the bank."

"Dear me, it does look suspicious!" remarked Armstrong.

"If Luke was guiding you to the train, I will take his place, sir."

"Thank you, but perhaps I had better keep him with me, and cross-examine him a little. I suppose I can depend upon your keeping your eyes upon him, and letting me know of any suspicious conduct on his part?"

"Yes, sir, I will do it with pleasure," Randolph announced promptly. He felt sure that he had excited Mr. Armstrong's suspicions, and defeated any plans Luke might have cherished of getting in with the capitalist.

"Have you anything more to communicate?" asked Mr. Armstrong, politely.

"No, sir; I thought it best to put you on your guard."

"I quite appreciate your motives, Master Randolph. I shall

keep my eyes open henceforth, and hope in time to discover the real perpetrator of the robbery. Now, Luke."

"I have dished you, young fellow!" thought Randolph, with a triumphant glance at the unconscious Luke. He walked away in high self-satisfaction.

"Luke," said Mr. Armstrong, as they resumed their walk, "Randolph seems a very warm friend of yours."

"I never thought so," said Luke, with an answering smile. "I am glad if he has changed."

"What arrangements do you think I have made with him?"

"I don't know, sir."

"I have asked him to keep his eye on you, and, if he sees anything suspicious, to let me know."

Luke would have been disturbed by this remark, had not the smile on Mr. Armstrong's face belied his words.

"Does he think you are in earnest, sir?"

"Oh, yes, he has no doubt of it. He warned me of your character, and said he was quite sure that you and your friend Mr. Reed were implicated in the bank robbery. I told him I would cross-examine you, and see what I could find out. Randolph told me that you were only a working boy, which I pronounced to be very much against you."

Luke laughed outright.

"I think you are fond of a practical joke, Mr. Armstrong," he said. "You have fooled Randolph very neatly."

"I had an object in it," said Mr. Armstrong quietly. "I may have occasion to employ you in the matter, and if so, it will be well that no arrangement is suspected between us. Randolph will undoubtedly inform his father of what happened this morning."

"As I said before, sir, I am ready to do anything that lies in my power."

Luke could not help feeling curious as to the character of the service he would be called upon to perform. He found it difficult to hazard a conjecture, but one thing at least seemed clear, and this was that Mr. Armstrong was disposed to be his friend, and as he was a rich man his friendship was likely to amount to something.

They had now reached the depot, and in ten minutes the train was due.

"Don't wait if you wish to get to work, Luke," said Mr. Armstrong kindly.

"My work can wait; it is nearly finished," said Luke.

The ten minutes passed rapidly, and with a cordial good-bye, the capitalist entered the train, leaving Luke to return to his modest home in good spirits.

"I have two influential friends, now," he said to himself—"Mr. Reed and Mr. Armstrong. On the whole, Luke Larkin, you are in luck, your prospects look decidedly bright, even if you have lost the janitorship."

CHAPTER XXIII

RANDOLPH AND HIS CREDITOR

THOUGH Randolph was pleased at having, as he thought, put a spoke in Luke's wheel, and filled Mr. Armstrong's mind with suspicion, he was not altogether happy. He had a little private trouble of his own. He had now for some time been a frequenter of Tony Denton's billiard saloon, patronizing both the table and the bar. He had fallen in with a few young men of no social standing, who flattered him, and, therefore, stood in his good graces. With them he played billiards and drank. After a time he found that he was exceeding his allowance, but in the most obliging way Tony Denton had offered him credit.

"Of course, Mr. Duncan"—Randolph felt flattered at being addressed in this way—"of course, Mr. Duncan, your credit is good with me. If you haven't the ready money, and I know most young gentlemen are liable to be short, I will just keep an account, and you can settle at your convenience."

This seemed very obliging, but I am disposed to think that a boy's worst enemy is the one who makes it easy for him to run into debt. Randolph was not wholly without caution, for he said: "But suppose, Tony, I am not able to pay when you want the money?"

"Oh, don't trouble yourself about that, Mr. Duncan," said Tony cordially. "Of course, I know the standing of your family, and I am perfectly safe. Some time you will be a rich man."

"Yes, I suppose I shall," said Randolph, in a consequential tone.

"And it is worth something to me to have my saloon patronized by a young gentleman of your social standing."

Evidently, Tony Denton understood Randolph's weak point,

and played on it skillfully. He assumed an air of extra consequence, as he remarked condescendingly: "You are very obliging, Tony, and I shall not forget it."

Tony Denton laughed in his sleeve at the boy's vanity, but his manner was very respectful, and Randolph looked upon him as an humble friend and admirer.

"He is a sensible man, Tony; he understands what is due to my position," he said to himself.

After Denton's visit to New York with Prince Duncan, and the knowledge which he then acquired about the president of the Groveton Bank, he decided that the time had come to cut short Randolph's credit with him. The day of reckoning always comes in such cases, as I hope my young friends will fully understand. Debt is much more easily contracted than liquidated, and this Randolph found to his cost.

One morning he was about to start on a game of billiards, when Tony Denton called him aside.

"I would like to speak a word to you, Mr. Duncan," he said smoothly.

"All right, Tony," said Randolph, in a patronizing tone. "What can I do for you?"

"My rent comes due to-morrow, Mr. Duncan, and I should be glad if you would pay me a part of your account. It has been running some time——"

Randolph's jaw fell, and he looked blank.

"How much do I owe you?" he asked.

Tony referred to a long ledgerlike account-book, turned to a certain page, and running his fingers down a long series of items, answered, "Twenty-seven dollars and sixty cents."

"It can't be so much!" ejaculated Randolph, in dismay. "Surely you have made a mistake!"

"You can look for yourself," said Tony suavely. "Just reckon it up; I may have made a little mistake in the sum total."

Randolph looked over the items, but he was nervous, and the page swam before his eyes. He was quite incapable of performing the addition, simple as it was, in his then frame of mind.

"I dare say you have added it up all right," he said, after an abortive attempt to reckon it up, "but I can hardly believe that I owe you so much."

" 'Many a little makes a mickle,' as we Scotch say," answered Tony cheerfully. "However, twenty-seven dollars is a mere trifle to a young man like you. Come, if you'll pay me to-night, I'll knock off the sixty cents."

"It's quite impossible for me to do it," said Randolph, ill at ease.

"Pay me something on account—say ten dollars."

"I haven't got but a dollar and a quarter in my pocket."

"Oh, well, you know where to go for more money," said Tony, with a wink. "The old gentleman's got plenty."

"I am not so sure about that—I mean that he is willing to pay out. Of course, he's got plenty of money invested," added Randolph, who liked to have it thought that his father was a great financial magnate.

"Well, he can spare some for his son, I am sure."

"Can't you let it go for a little while longer, Tony?" asked Randolph, awkwardly.

"Really, Mr. Duncan, I couldn't. I am a poor man, as you know, and have my bills to pay."

"I take it as very disobliging, Tony; I sha'n't care to patronize your place any longer," said Randolph, trying a new tack.

Tony Denton shrugged his shoulders.

"I only care for patrons who are willing to pay their bills," he answered significantly. "It doesn't pay me to keep my place open free."

"Of course not; but I hope you are not afraid of me?"

"Certainly not. I am sure you will act honorably and pay your bills. If I thought you wouldn't, I would go and see your father about it."

"No, you mustn't do that," said Randolph, alarmed. "He doesn't know I come here."

"And he won't know from me, if you pay what you owe."

Matters were becoming decidedly unpleasant for Randolph. The perspiration gathered on his brow. He didn't know what to do. That his father would not give him money for any such purpose, he very well knew, and he dreaded his finding out where he spent so many of his evenings.

"Oh, don't trouble yourself about a trifle," said Tony smoothly. "Just go up to your father, frankly, and tell him you want the money."

"He wouldn't give me twenty-seven dollars," said Randolph gloomily.

"Then ask for ten, and I'll wait for the balance till next week."

"Can't you put it all off till next week?"

"No; I really couldn't, Mr. Duncan. What does it matter to you this week, or next?"

Randolph wished to put off as long as possible the inevitable moment, though he knew it would do him no good in the end. But Tony Denton was inflexible—and he finally said: "Well, I'll make the attempt, but I know I shall fail."

"That's all right; I knew you would look at it in the right light. Now, go ahead and play your game."

"No, I don't want to increase my debt."

"Oh, I won't charge you for what you play this evening. Tony Denton can be liberal as well as the next man. Only I have to collect money to pay my bills."

Randolph didn't know that all this had been prearranged by the obliging saloon-keeper, and that, in now pressing him, he had his own object in view.

The next morning, Randolph took an opportunity to see his father alone.

"Father," he said, "will you do me a favor?"

"What is it, Randolph?"

"Let me have ten dollars."

His father frowned.

"What do you want with ten dollars?" he asked.

"I don't like to go round without money in my pocket. It doesn't look well for the son of a rich man."

"Who told you I was a rich man?" said his father testily.

"Why, you are, aren't you? Everybody in the village says so."

"I may, or may not, be rich, but I don't care to encourage my son in extravagant habits. You say you have no money. Don't you have your regular allowance?"

"It is only two dollars a week."

"Only two dollars a week!" repeated the father angrily. "Let me tell you, young man, that when I was of your age I didn't have twenty-five cents a week."

"That was long ago. People lived differently from what they do now."

"How did they?"

"They didn't live in any style."

"They didn't spend money foolishly, as they do now. I don't see for my part what you can do with even two dollars a week."

"Oh, it melts away, one way or another. I am your only son,

and people expect me to spend money. It is expected of one in my position."

"So you can. I consider two dollars a week very liberal."

"You'd understand better if you were a young fellow like me how hard it is to get along on that."

"I don't want to understand," returned his father stoutly. "One thing I understand, and that is, that the boys of the present day are foolishly extravagant. Think of Luke Larkin! Do you think he spends two dollars even in a month?"

"I hope you don't mean to compare me with a working boy like Luke?" Randolph said scornfully.

"I am not sure but Luke would suit me better than you in some respects."

"You are speaking of Luke," said Randolph, with a lucky thought. "Well, even he, working boy as he is, has a better watch than I, who am the son of the president of the Groveton Bank."

"Do you want the ten dollars to buy a better watch?" asked Prince Duncan.

"Yes," answered Randolph, ready to seize on any pretext for the sake of getting the money.

"Then wait till I go to New York again, and I will look at some watches. I won't make any promise, but I may buy you one. I don't care about Luke outshining you."

This by no means answered Randolph's purpose.

"Won't you let me go up to the city myself, father?" he asked.

"No, I prefer to rely upon my own judgment in a purchase of that kind."

It had occurred to Randolph that he would go to the city, and pretend on his return that he had bought a watch but had his pocket picked. Of course, his father would give him more than ten dollars for the purpose, and he could privately pay it over to Tony Denton.

But this scheme did not work, and he made up his mind at last that he would have to tell Tony he must wait.

He did so. Tony Denton, who fully expected this, and, for reasons of his own, did not regret it, said very little to Randolph, but decided to go round and see Prince Duncan himself. It would give him a chance to introduce the other and more important matter.

It was about this time that Linton's birthday-party took

place. Randolph knew, of course, that he would meet Luke, but he no longer had the satisfaction of deriding his shabby dress. Our hero wore his best suit, and showed as much ease and self-possession as Randolph himself.

"What airs that boy Luke puts on!" ejaculated Randolph, in disgust. "I believe he thinks he is my equal."

In this Randolph was correct. Luke certainly did consider himself the social equal of the haughty Randolph, and the consciousness of being well dressed made him feel at greater ease than at Florence Grant's party. He had taken additional lessons in dancing from his friend Linton, and, being quick to learn, showed no awkwardness on the floor. Linton's parents, by their kind cordiality, contributed largely to the pleasure of their son's guests, who at the end of the evening unanimously voted the party a success.

CHAPTER XXIV

A COMMISSION FOR LUKE

UPON his return to the city, John Armstrong lost no time in sending for Roland Reed. The latter, though rather surprised at the summons, answered it promptly. When he entered the office of the old merchant he found him sitting at his desk.

"Mr. Armstrong?" he said inquiringly.

"That's my name. You, I take it, are Roland Reed."

"Yes."

"No doubt you wonder why I sent for you," said Mr. Armstrong.

"Is it about the robbery of the Groveton Bank?"

"You have guessed it. You know, I suppose, that I am the owner of the missing box of bonds?"

"So I was told. Have you obtained any clue?"

"I have not had time. I have only just returned from Europe. I have done nothing except visit Groveton."

"What led you to send for me? Pardon my curiosity, but I can't help asking."

"An interview with a protégé of yours, Luke Larkin."

"You know that Luke was arrested on suspicion of being

connected with the robbery, though there are those who pay me the compliment of thinking that I may have had something to do with it."

"I think you had as much to do with it as Luke Larkin," said Armstrong, deliberately.

"I had—just as much," said Reed, with a smile. "Luke is a good boy, Mr. Armstrong."

"I quite agree with you. If I had a son I should like him to resemble Luke."

"Give me your hand on that, Mr. Armstrong," said Roland Reed, impulsively. "Excuse my impetuosity, but I've taken a fancy to that boy."

"There, then, we are agreed. Now, Mr. Reed, I will tell you why I have taken the liberty of sending for you. From what Luke said, I judged that you were a sharp, shrewd man of the world, and might help me in this matter, which I confess puzzles me. You know the particulars, and therefore, without preamble, I am going to ask you whether you have any theory as regards this robbery. The box hasn't walked off without help. Now, who took it from the bank?"

"If I should tell you my suspicion you might laugh at me."

"I will promise not to do that."

"Then I believe that Prince Duncan, president of the Groveton Bank, could tell you, if he chose, what has become of the box."

"Extraordinary!" ejaculated John Armstrong.

"I supposed you would be surprised—probably indignant, if you are a friend of Duncan—but, nevertheless, I adhere to my statement."

"You mistake the meaning of my exclamation. I spoke of it as extraordinary, because the same suspicion has entered my mind, though, I admit, without a special reason."

"I have a reason."

"May I inquire what it is?"

"I knew Prince Duncan when he was a young man, though he does not know me now. In fact, I may as well admit that I was then known by another name. He wronged me deeply at that time, being guilty of a crime which he successfully laid upon my shoulders. No one in Groveton—no one of his recent associates—knows the real nature of the man as well as I do."

"You prefer not to go into particulars?"

"Not at present."

"At all events you can give me your advice. To suspect amounts to little. We must bring home the crime to him. It is here that I need your advice."

"I understand that the box contained government bonds."

"Yes."

"What were the denominations?"

"One ten thousand dollar bond, one five, and ten of one thousand each."

"It seems to me they ought to be traced. I suppose, of course, they were coupon, not registered."

"You are right. Had they been registered, I should have been at no trouble, nor would the thief have reaped any advantage."

"If coupon, they are, of course, numbered. Won't that serve as a clue, supposing an attempt is made to dispose of them?"

"You touch the weak point of my position. They are numbered, and I had a list of the numbers, but that list has disappeared. It is either lost or mislaid. Of course, I can't identify them."

"That is awkward. Wouldn't the banker of whom you bought them be able to give you the numbers?"

"Yes, but I don't know where they were bought. I had at the time in my employ a clerk and book-keeper, a steady-going and methodical man of fifty-odd, who made the purchase, and no doubt has a list of the numbers of the bonds."

"Then where is your difficulty?" asked Roland Reed, in surprise. "Go to the clerk and put the question. What can be simpler?"

"But I don't know where he is."

"Don't know where he is?" echoed Reed, in genuine surprise.

"No; James Harding—this is his name—left my employ a year since, having, through a life of economy, secured a competence, and went out West to join a widowed sister who had for many years made her residence there. Now, the West is a large place, and I don't know where this sister lives, or where James Harding is to be found."

"Yet he must be found. You must send a messenger to look for him."

"But whom shall I send? In a matter of this delicacy I don't want to employ a professional detective. Those men sometimes betray secrets committed to their keeping, and work up a false clue rather than have it supposed they are not earning their money. If, now, some gentleman in whom I had confidence—someone like yourself—would undertake the commission, I should esteem myself fortunate."

"Thank you for the compliment, Mr. Armstrong, more especially as you are putting confidence in a stranger, but I have important work to do that would not permit me to leave New York at present. But I know of someone whom I would employ, if the business were mine."

"Well?"

"Luke Larkin."

"But he is only a boy. He can't be over sixteen."

"He is a sharp boy, however, and would follow instructions."

John Armstrong thought rapidly. He was a man who decided quickly.

"I will take your advice," he said. "As I don't want to have it supposed that he is in my employ, will you oblige me by writing to him and preparing him for a journey? Let it be supposed that he is occupied with a commission for you."

"I will attend to the matter at once."

The next morning Luke received the following letter:

"MY DEAR LUKE: I have some work for you which will occupy some time and require a journey. You will be well paid. Bring a supply of underclothing, and assure your mother that she need feel under no apprehensions about you. Unless I am greatly mistaken, you will be able to take care of yourself.

"Your friend,
"ROLAND REED."

Luke read the letter with excitement and pleasure. He was to go on a journey, and to a boy of his age a journey of any sort is delightful. He had no idea of the extent of the trip in store for him, but thought he might possibly be sent to Boston, or Philadelphia, and either trip he felt would yield him much pleasure. He quieted the natural apprehensions of his mother, and, satchel in hand, waited upon his patron in the course of a day. By him he was taken over to the office of Mr. Armstrong, from whom he received instructions and a supply of money.

CHAPTER XXV

MR. J. MADISON COLEMAN

LUKE didn't shrink from the long trip before him. He enjoyed the prospect of it, having always longed to travel and see distant places. He felt flattered by Mr. Armstrong's confidence in him, and stoutly resolved to deserve it. He would have been glad if he could have had the company of his friend Linton, but he knew that this was impossible. He must travel alone.

"You have a difficult and perplexing task, Luke," said the capitalist. "You may not succeed."

"I will do my best, Mr. Armstrong."

"That is all I have a right to expect. If you succeed, you will do me a great service, of which I shall show proper appreciation."

He gave Luke some instructions, and it was arranged that our hero should write twice a week, and, if occasion required, oftener, so that his employer might be kept apprised of his movements.

Luke was not to stop short of Chicago. There his search was to begin; and there, if possible, he was to obtain information that might guide his subsequent steps.

It is a long ride to Chicago, as Luke found. He spent a part of the time in reading, and a part in looking out of the window at the scenery, but still, at times, he felt lonely.

"I wish Linton Tomkins were with me," he reflected. "What a jolly time we would have!"

But Linton didn't even know what had become of his friend. Luke's absence was an occasion for wonder at Groveton, and many questions were asked of his mother.

"He was sent for by Mr. Reed," answered the widow. "He is at work for him."

"Mr. Reed is in New York, isn't he?"

"Yes."

It was concluded, therefore, that Luke was in New York, and one or two persons proposed to call upon him there, but his mother professed ignorance of his exact residence. She knew that he was traveling, but even she was kept in the dark as to where he was, nor did she know that Mr. Armstrong, and not Mr. Reed, was his employer.

Some half dozen hours before reaching Chicago, a young man of twenty-five, or thereabouts, sauntered along the aisle, and sat down in the vacant seat beside Luke.

"Nice day," he said, affably.

"Very nice," responded Luke.

"I suppose you are bound to Chicago?"

"Yes, I expect to stay there awhile."

"Going farther?"

"I can't tell yet."

"Going to school out there?"

"No."

"Perhaps you are traveling for some business firm, though you look pretty young for that."

"No, I'm not a drummer, if that's what you mean. Still, I have a commisison from a New York business man."

"A commission—of what kind?" drawled the newcomer.

"It is of a confidential character," said Luke.

"Ha! close-mouthed," thought the young man. "Well, I'll get it out of him after awhile."

He didn't press the question, not wishing to arouse suspicion or mistrust.

"Just so," he replied. "You are right to keep it to yourself, though you wouldn't mind trusting me if you knew me better. Is this your first visit to Chicago?"

"Yes, sir."

"Suppose we exchange cards. This is mine."

He handed Luke a card, bearing this name:

J. MADISON COLEMAN

At the bottom of the card he wrote in pencil, "representing H. B. Claflin & Co."

"Of course you've heard of our firm," he said.

"Certainly."

"I don't have the firm name printed on my card, for Claflin won't allow it. You will notice that I am called for old President Madison. He was an old friend of my grandfather. In fact, grandfather held a prominent office under his administration—collector of the port of New York."

"I have no card with me," responded Luke. "But my name is Luke Larkin."

"Good name. Do you live in New York?"

"No; a few miles in the country."

"And whom do you represent?"

"Myself for the most part," answered Luke, with a smile.

"Good! No one has a better right to. I see there's something in you, Luke."

"You've found it out pretty quick," thought Luke.

"And I hope we will get better acquainted. If you're not permanently employed by this party, whose name you don't give, I will get you into the employ of Claflin & Co., if you would like it."

"Thank you," answered Luke, who thought it quite possible that he might like to obtain a position with so eminent a firm. "How long have you been with them?"

"Ten years—ever since I was of your age," promptly answered Mr. Coleman.

"Is promotion rapid?" Luke asked, with interest.

"Well, that depends on a man's capacity. I have been pushed right along. I went there as a boy, on four dollars a week; now I'm a traveling salesman—drummer as it is called—and I make about four thousand a year."

"That's a fine salary," said Luke, feeling that his new acquaintance must be possessed of extra ability to occupy so desirable a position.

"Yes, but I expect next year to get five thousand—Claflin knows I am worth it, and as he is a liberal man, I guess he will give it sooner than let me go."

"I suppose many do not get on so well, Mr. Coleman."

"I should say so! Now, there is a young fellow went there the same time that I did—his name is Frank Bolton. We were schoolfellows together, and just the same age, that is, nearly—he was born in April, and I in May. Well, we began at the same time on the same salary. Now I get sixty dollars a week and he only twelve—and he is glad to get that, too."

"I suppose he hasn't much business capacity."

"That's where you've struck it, Luke. He knows about enough to be clerk in a country store—and I suppose he'll fetch up there some day. You know what that means—selling sugar, and tea, and dried apples to old ladies, and occasionally measuring off a yard of calico, or selling a spool of cotton. If I couldn't do better than that I'd hire out as a farm laborer."

Luke smiled at the enumeration of the duties of a country salesman. It was clear that Mr. Coleman, though he looked city-bred, must at some time in the past have lived in the country.

"Perhaps that is the way I should turn out," he said. "I might not rise any higher than your friend Mr. Bolton."

"Oh, yes, you would. You're smart enough, I'll guarantee. You might not get on so fast as I have, for it isn't every young man of twenty-six that can command four thousand dollars a year, but you would rise to a handsome income, I am sure."

"I should be satisfied with two thousand a year at your age."

"I would be willing to guarantee you that," asserted Mr. Coleman, confidently. "By the way, where do you propose to put up in Chicago?"

"I have not decided yet."

"You'd better go with me to the Ottawa House."

"Is it a good house?"

"They'll feed you well there, and only charge two dollars a day."

"Is it centrally located?"

"It isn't as central as the Palmer, or Sherman, or Tremont, but it is convenient to everything."

I ought to say here that I have chosen to give a fictitious name to the hotel designated by Mr. Coleman.

"Come, what do you say?"

"I have no objection," answered Luke, after a slight pause for reflection.

Indeed, it was rather pleasant to him to think that he would have a companion on his first visit to Chicago who was well acquainted with the city, and could serve as his guide. Though he should not feel justified in imparting to Mr. Coleman his special business, he meant to see something of the city, and would find his new friend a pleasant companion.

"That's good," said Coleman, well pleased. "I shall be glad to have your company. I expected to meet a friend on the train, but something must have delayed him, and so I should have been left alone."

"I suppose a part of your time will be given to business?" suggested Luke.

"Yes, but I take things easy; when I work, I work. I can

accomplish as much in a couple of hours as many would do in a whole day. You see, I understand my customers. When soft sawder is wanted, I am soft sawder. When I am dealing with a plain, businesslike man, I talk in a plain, businesslike way. I study my man, and generally I succeed in striking him for an order, even if times are hard and he is already well stocked."

"He certainly knows how to talk," thought Luke. In fact, he was rather disposed to accept Mr. Coleman at his own valuation, though that was a very high one.

"Do you smoke?"

"Not at all."

"Not even a cigarette?"

"Not even a cigarette."

"I was intending to ask you to go with me into the smoking-car for a short time. I smoke a good deal; it is my only vice. You know we must all have some vices."

Luke didn't see the necessity, but he assented, because it seemed to be expected.

"I won't be gone long. You'd better come along, too, and smoke a cigarette. It is time you began to smoke. Most boys begin much earlier."

Luke shook his head.

"I don't care to learn," he said.

"Oh, you're a good boy--one of the Sunday-school kind," said Coleman, with a slight sneer. "You'll get over that after a while. You'll be here when I come back?"

Luke promised that he would, and for the next half hour he was left alone. As his friend Mr. Coleman left the car, he followed him with his glance, and surveyed him more attentively than he had hitherto done. The commercial traveler was attired in a suit of fashionable plaid, wore a showy necktie, from the center of which blazed a diamond scarfpin. A showy chain crossed his vest, and to it was appended a large and showy watch, which looked valuable, though appearances are sometimes deceitful.

"He must spend a good deal of money," thought Luke. "I wonder that he should be willing to go to a two-dollar-a-day hotel."

Luke, for his own part, was quite willing to go to the Ottawa House. He had never fared luxuriously, and he had no doubt that even at the Ottawa House he should live better than at home.

It was nearer an hour than half an hour before Coleman came back.

"I stayed away longer than I intended," he said. "I smoked three cigars, instead of one, seeing you wasn't with me to keep me company. I found some social fellows, and we had a chat."

Mr. Coleman absented himself once or twice more. Finally, the train ran into the depot, and the conductor called out, "Chicago!"

"Come along, Luke!" said Coleman.

The two left the car in company. Coleman hailed a cab—gave the order, Ottawa House—and in less than five minutes they were rattling over the pavements toward their hotel.

CHAPTER XXVI

THE OTTAWA HOUSE

THERE was one little circumstance that led Luke to think favorably of his new companion. As the hackman closed the door of the carriage, Luke asked: "How much is the fare?"

"Fifty cents apiece, gentlemen," answered cabby.

Luke was about to put his hand into his pocket for the money, when Coleman touching him on the arm, said: "Never mind, Luke, I have the money," and before our hero could expostulate he had thrust a dollar into the cab-driver's hand.

"All right, thanks," said the driver, and slammed to the door.

"You must let me repay you my part of the fare, Mr. Coleman," said Luke, again feeling for his pocketbook.

"Oh, it's a mere trifle!" said Coleman. "I'll let you pay next time, but don't be so ceremonious with a friend."

"But I would rather pay for myself," objected Luke.

"Oh, say no more about it, I beg. Claflin provides liberally for my expenses. It's all right."

"But I don't want Claflin to pay for me."

"Then I assure you I'll get it out of you before we part. Will that content you?"

Luke let the matter drop, but he didn't altogether like to find himself under obligations to a stranger, notwithstanding his assurance, which he took for a joke. He would have been surprised and startled if he had known how thoroughly Coleman meant what he said about getting even. The fifty cents he had with such apparent generosity paid out for Luke he meant to get back a hundred-fold. His object was to gain Luke's entire confidence, and remove any suspicion he might possibly entertain. In this respect he was successful. Luke had read about designing strangers, but he certainly could not suspect a man who insisted on paying his hack fare.

"I hope you will not be disappointed in the Ottawa House," observed Mr. Coleman, as they rattled through the paved streets. "It isn't a stylish hotel."

"I am not used to stylish living," said Luke, frankly. "I have always been used to living in a very plain way."

"When I first went on the road I used to stop at the tip-top houses, such as the Palmer at Chicago, the Russell House in Detroit, etc., but it's useless extravagance. Claflin allows me a generous sum for hotels, and if I go to a cheap one, I put the difference into my own pocket."

"Is that expected?" asked Luke, doubtfully.

"It's allowed, at any rate. No one can complain if I choose to live a little plainer. When it pays in the way of business to stop at a big hotel, I do so. Of course, your boss pays your expenses?"

"Yes."

"Then you'd better do as I do—put the difference in your own pocket."

"I shouldn't like to do that."

"Why not? It is evident you are a new traveler, or you would know that it is a regular thing."

Luke did not answer, but he adhered to his own view. He meant to keep a careful account of his disbursements and report to Mr. Armstrong, without the addition of a single penny. He had no doubt that he should be paid liberally for his time, and he didn't care to make anything by extra means.

The Ottawa House was nearly a mile and a half distant. It was on one of the lower streets, near the lake. It was a plain building with accommodations for perhaps a hundred and fifty guests. This would be large for a country town or small city, but it indicated a hotel of the third class in Chicago. I may as well say here, however, that it was a perfectly respectable and honestly conducted hotel, notwithstanding it was selected by Mr. Coleman, who could not with truth be complimented so highly. I will also add that Mr. Coleman's selection of the Ottawa, in place of a more pretentious hotel, arose from the fear that in the latter he might meet someone who knew him, and who would warn Luke of his undesirable reputation.

Jumping out of the hack, J. Madison Coleman led the way into the hotel, and, taking pen in hand, recorded his name in large, flourishing letters—as from New York.

Then he handed the pen to Luke, who registered himself also from New York.

"Give us a room together," he said to the clerk.

Luke did not altogether like this arrangement, but hardly felt like objecting. He did not wish to hurt the feelings of J. Madison Coleman, yet he considered that, having known him only six hours, it was somewhat imprudent to allow such intimacy. But he who hesitates is lost, and before Luke had made up his mind whether to object or not, he was already part way upstairs—there was no elevator—following the bellboy, who carried his luggage.

The room, which was on the fourth floor, was of good size, and contained two beds. So far so good. After the ride he wished to wash and put on clean clothes. Mr. Coleman did not think this necessary, and saying to Luke that he would find him downstairs, he left our hero alone.

"I wish I had a room alone," thought Luke. "I should like it much better, but I don't want to offend Coleman. I've got eighty dollars in my pocketbook, and though, of course, he is all right, I don't want to take any risks."

On the door he read the regulations of the hotel. One item attracted his attention. It was this:

"The proprietors wish distinctly to state that they will not be responsible for money or valuables unless left with the clerk to be deposited in the safe."

Luke had not been accustomed to stopping at hotels, and did not know that this was the usual custom. It struck him, however, as an excellent arrangement, and he resolved to avail himself of it.

When he went downstairs he didn't see Mr. Coleman.

"Your friend has gone out," said the clerk. "He wished me to say that he would be back in half an hour."

"All right," answered Luke. "Can I leave my pocketbook with you?"

"Certainly."

The clerk wrapped it up in a piece of brown paper and put it away in the safe at the rear of the office, marking it with Luke's name and the number of his room.

"There, that's safe!" thought Luke, with a feeling of relief. He had reserved about three dollars, as he might have occasion to spend a little money in the course of the evening. If he were robbed of this small amount it would not much matter.

A newsboy came in with an evening paper. Luke bought a copy and sat down on a bench in the office, near a window. He was reading busily, when someone tapped him on the shoulder. Looking up, he saw that it was his roommate, J. Madison Coleman.

"I've just been taking a little walk," he said, "and now I am ready for dinner. If you are, too, let us go into the dining-room."

Luke was glad to accept this proposal, his long journey having given him a good appetite.

CHAPTER XXVII

COLEMAN ACTS SUSPICIOUSLY

AFTER dinner, Coleman suggested a game of billiards, but as this was a game with which Luke was not familiar, he declined the invitation, but went into the billiard-room and watched a game between his new acquaintance and a stranger. Coleman proved to be a very good player, and won the game. After the first game Coleman called for drinks, and invited Luke to join them.

"Thank you," answered Luke, "but I never drink."

"Oh, I forgot; you're a good boy," said Coleman. "Well, I'm no Puritan. Whisky straight for me."

Luke was not in the least troubled by the sneer conveyed in Coleman's words. He was not altogether entitled to credit for refusing to drink, having not the slightest taste for strong drink of any kind.

About half-past seven Coleman put up his cue, saying: "That'll do for me. Now, Luke, suppose we take a walk."

Luke was quite ready, not having seen anything of Chicago as yet. They strolled out, and walked for an hour. Coleman, to do him justice, proved an excellent guide, and pointed out whatever they passed which was likely to interest his young companion. But at last he seemed to be tired.

"It's only half-past eight," he said, referring to his watch. "I'll drop into some theater. It is the best way to finish up the evening."

"Then I'll go back to the hotel," said Luke. "I feel tired, and mean to go to bed early."

"You'd better spend an hour or two in the theater with me."

"No, I believe not. I prefer a good night's rest."

"Do you mind my leaving you?"

"Not at all."

"Can you find your way back to the hotel alone?"

"If you'll direct me, I think I can find it."

The direction was given, and Coleman was turning off, when, as if it had just occurred to him, he said: "By the way, can you lend me a five? I've nothing less than a fifty-dollar bill with me, and I don't want to break that."

Luke congratulated himself now that he had left the greater part of his money at the hotel.

"I can let you have a dollar," he said.

Coleman shrugged his shoulders, but answered: "All right; let me have the one."

Luke did so, and felt now that he had more than repaid the fifty cents his companion had paid for hack fare. Though Coleman had professed to have nothing less than fifty, Luke knew that he had changed a five-dollar bill at the hotel in paying for the drinks, and must have over four dollars with him in small bills and change.

"Why, then," thought he, "did Coleman want to borrow five dollars of me?"

If Luke had known more of the world he would have understood that it was only one of the tricks to which men like Coleman resort to obtain a loan, or rather a gift, from an unsuspecting acquaintance.

"I suppose I shall not see my money back," thought Luke. "Well, it will be the last that he will get out of me."

He was already becoming tired of his companion, and doubted whether he would not find the acquaintance an expensive one. He was sorry that they were to share the same room. However, it was for one night only, and to-morrow he was quite resolved to part company.

Shortly after nine o'clock Luke went to bed, and being fatigued with his long journey, was soon asleep. He was still sleeping at twelve o'clock, when Coleman came home.

Coleman came up to his bed and watched him attentively.

"The kid's asleep," he soliloquized. "He's one of the good Sunday-school boys. I can imagine how shocked he would be if he knew that, instead of being a traveler for H. B. Claflin, I have been living by my wits for the last half-dozen years. He seems to be half asleep. I think I can venture to explore a little."

He took Luke's trousers from the chair on which he had laid them, and thrust his fingers into the pockets, but brought forth only a penknife and a few pennies.

"He keeps his money somewhere else, it seems," said Coleman.

Next he turned to the vest, and from the inside vest pocket drew out Luke's modest pocketbook.

"Oh, here we have it," thought Coleman, with a smile. "Cunning boy; he thought nobody would think of looking in his vest pocket. Well, let us see how much he has got."

He opened the pocketbook, and frowned with disappointment when he discovered only a two-dollar bill.

"What does it mean? Surely he hasn't come to Chicago with only this paltry sum!" exclaimed Coleman. "He must be more cunning than I thought."

He looked in the coat pockets, the shoes, and even the socks of his young companion, but found nothing, except the silver watch, which Luke had left in one of his vest pockets.

"Confound the boy! He's foiled me this time!" muttered Coleman. "Shall I take the watch? No; it might expose me, and I could not raise much on it at the pawnbroker's. He must have left his money with the clerk downstairs. He wouldn't think of it himself, but probably he was advised to do so before he left home. I'll get up early, and see if I can't get in ahead of my young friend."

Coleman did not venture to take the two-dollar bill, as that would have induced suspicion on the part of Luke, and would have interfered with his intention of securing the much larger sum of money, which, as he concluded rightly, was in the safe in the office.

He undressed and got into bed, but not without observation. As he was bending over Luke's clothes, examining them, our hero's eyes suddenly opened, and he saw what was going on. It flashed upon him at once what kind of a companion he had fallen in with, but he had the wisdom and self-control to close his eyes again immediately. He reflected that there was not much that Coleman could take, and if he took the watch he resolved to charge him openly with it. To make a disturbance there and then might be dangerous, as Coleman, who was much stronger than he, might ill-treat and abuse him, without his being able to offer any effectual resistance.

CHAPTER XXVIII

COLEMAN'S LITTLE PLAN

THOUGH Coleman went to bed late, he awoke early. He had the power of awaking at almost any hour that he might fix. He was still quite fatigued, but having an object in view, overcame his tendency to lie longer, and swiftly dressing himself, went downstairs. Luke was still sleeping, and did not awaken while his companion was dressing.

Coleman went downstairs and strolled up to the clerk's desk.

"You're up early," said that official.

"Yes, it's a great nuisance, but I have a little business to attend to with a man who leaves Chicago by an early train. I tried to find him last night, but he had probably gone to some theater. That is what has forced me to get up so early this morning."

"I am always up early," said the clerk.

"Then you are used to it, and don't mind it. It is different with me."

Coleman bought a cigar, and while he was lighting it, remarked, as if incidentally:

"By the way, did my young friend leave my money with you last evening?"

"He left a package of money with me, but he didn't mention it was yours."

"Forgot to, I suppose. I told him to leave it here, as I was going out to the theater, and was afraid I might have my pocket picked. Smart fellows, those pickpockets. I claim to be rather smart myself, but there are some of them smart enough to get ahead of me.

"I was relieved of my pocketbook containing over two hundred dollars in money once. By Jove! I was mad enough to knock the fellow's head off, if I had caught him."

"It is rather provoking."

"I think I'll trouble you to hand me the money the boy left with you, as I have to use some this morning."

Mr. Coleman spoke in an easy, off-hand way, that might have taken in some persons, but hotel clerks are made smart by their positions.

"I am sorry, Mr. Coleman," said the clerk, "but I can only give it back to the boy."

"I commend your caution, my friend," said Coleman, "but I can assure you that it's all right. I sent it back by Luke when I was going to the theater, and I meant, of course, to have him give my name with it. However, he is not used to business, and so forgot it."

"When did you hand it to him?" asked the clerk, with new-born suspicion.

"About eight o'clock. No doubt he handed it in as soon as he came back to the hotel."

"How much was there?"

This question posed Mr. Coleman, as he had no idea how much money Luke had with him.

"I can't say exactly," he answered. "I didn't count it. There might have been seventy-five dollars, though perhaps the sum fell a little short of that."

"I can't give you the money, Mr. Coleman," said the clerk, briefly. "I have no evidence that it is yours."

"Really, that's ludicrous," said Coleman, with a forced laugh. "You don't mean to doubt me, I hope," and Madison Coleman drew himself up haughtily.

"That has nothing to do with it. The rule of this office is to return money only to the person who deposited it with us. If we adopted any other rule, we should get into no end of trouble."

"But, my friend," said Coleman, frowning, "you are putting me to great inconvenience. I must meet my friend in twenty minutes and pay him a part of this money."

"I have nothing to do with that," said the clerk.

"You absolutely refuse, then?"

"I do," answered the clerk, firmly. "However, you can easily overcome the difficulty by bringing the boy down here to authorize me to hand you the money."

"It seems to me that you have plenty of red tape here," said

Coleman, shrugging his shoulders. "However, I must do as you require."

Coleman had a bright thought, which he proceeded to carry into execution.

He left the office and went upstairs. He was absent long enough to visit the chamber which he and Luke had occupied together. Then he reported to the office again.

"The boy is not dressed," he said, cheerfully. "However, he has given me an order for the money, which, of course, will do as well."

He handed a paper, the loose leaf of a memorandum book, on which were written in pencil these words:

"Give my guardian, Mr. Coleman, the money I left on deposit at the office. LUKE LARKIN."

"That makes it all right, doesn't it?" asked Coleman, jauntily. "Now, if you'll be kind enough to hand me my money at once, I'll be off."

"It won't do, Mr. Coleman," said the clerk. "How am I to know that the boy wrote this?"

"Don't you see his signature?"

The clerk turned to the hotel register, where Luke had enrolled his name.

"The handwriting is not the same," he said, coldly.

"Oh, confound it!" exclaimed Coleman, testily. "Can't you understand that writing with a pencil makes a difference?"

"I understand," said the clerk, "that you are trying to get money that does not belong to you. The money was deposited a couple of hours sooner than the time you claim to have handed it to the boy—just after you and the boy arrived."

"You're right," said Coleman, unabashed. "I made a mistake."

"You cannot have the money."

"You have no right to keep it from me," said Coleman, wrathfully.

"Bring the boy to the office and it shall be delivered to him; then, if he chooses to give it to you, I have nothing to say."

"But I tell you he is not dressed."

"He seems to be," said the clerk, quietly, with a glance at the door, through which Luke was just entering.

Coleman's countenance changed. He was now puzzled for

a moment. Then a bold plan suggested itself. He would charge Luke with having stolen the money from him.

CHAPTER XXIX

MR. COLEMAN IS FOILED IN HIS ATTEMPT

LUKE looked from Coleman to the clerk in some surprise. He saw from their looks that they were discussing some matter which concerned him.

"You left some money in my charge yesterday, Mr. Larkin," said the clerk.

"Yes."

"Your friend here claims it. Am I to give it to him?"

Luke's eyes lighted up indignantly.

"What does this mean, Mr. Coleman?" he demanded, sternly.

"It means," answered Coleman, throwing off the mask, "that the money is mine, and that you have no right to it."

If Luke had not witnessed Coleman's search of his pockets during the night, he would have been very much astonished at this brazen statement. As it was, he had already come to the conclusion that his railroad acquaintance was a sharper.

"I will trouble you to prove your claim to it," said Luke, not at all disturbed by Coleman's impudent assertion.

"I gave it to you yesterday to place in the safe. I did not expect you would put it in in your own name," continued Coleman, with brazen hardihood.

"When did you hand it to me?" asked Luke, calmly.

"When we first went up into the room."

This change in his original charge Coleman made in consequence of learning the time of the deposit.

"This is an utter falsehood!" exclaimed Luke, indignantly.

"Take care, young fellow!" blustered Coleman. "Your reputation for honesty isn't of the best. I don't like to expose you, but a boy who has served a three months' term in the penitentiary had better be careful how he acts."

Luke's breath was quite taken away by this unexpected attack. The clerk began to eye him with suspicion, so confident was Coleman's tone.

"Mr. Lawrence," said Luke, for he had learned the clerk's name, "will you allow me a word in private?"

"I object to this," said Coleman, in a blustering tone. "Whatever you have to say you can say before me."

"Yes," answered the clerk, who did not like Coleman's bullying tone, "I will hear what you have to say."

He led the way into an adjoining room, and assumed an air of attention.

"This man is a stranger to me," Luke commenced. "I saw him yesterday afternoon for the first time in my life."

"But he says he is your guardian."

"He is no more my guardian than you are. Indeed, I would much sooner select you."

"How did you get acquainted?"

"He introduced himself to me as a traveler for H. B. Claflin, of New York. I did not doubt his statement at the time, but now I do, especially after what happened in the night."

"What was that?" asked the clerk, pricking up his ears.

Luke went on to describe Coleman's search of his pockets.

"Did you say anything?"

"No. I wished to see what he was after. As I had left nearly all my money with you, I was not afraid of being robbed."

"I presume your story is correct. In fact, I detected him in a misstatement as to the time of giving you the money. But I don't want to get into trouble."

"Ask him how much money I deposited with you," suggested Luke. "He has no idea, and will have to guess."

"I have asked him the question once, but will do so again."

The clerk returned to the office with Luke. Coleman eyed them uneasily, as if he suspected them of having been engaged in a conspiracy against him.

"Well," he said, "are you going to give me my money?"

"State the amount," said the clerk, in a businesslike manner.

"I have already told you that I can't state exactly. I handed the money to Luke without counting it."

"You must have some idea, at any rate," said the clerk.

"Of course I have. There was somewhere around seventy-five dollars."

This he said with a confidence which he did not feel, for it was, of course, a mere guess.

"You are quite out in your estimate, Mr. Coleman. It is

evident to me that you have made a false claim. You will oblige me by settling your bill and leaving the hotel."

"Do you think I will submit to such treatment?" demanded Coleman, furiously.

"I think you'll have to," returned the clerk, quietly. "You can go in to breakfast, if you like, but you must afterward leave the hotel. John," this to a bellboy, "go up to number forty-seven and bring down this gentleman's luggage."

"You and the boy are in a conspiracy against me!" exclaimed Coleman, angrily. "I have a great mind to have you both arrested!"

"I advise you not to attempt it. You may get into trouble."

Coleman apparently did think better of it. Half an hour later he left the hotel, and Luke found himself alone. He decided that he must be more circumspect hereafter.

CHAPTER XXX

A DISCOVERY

LUKE was in Chicago, but what to do next he did not know. He might have advertised in one or more of the Chicago papers for James Harding, formerly in the employ of John Armstrong, of New York, but if this should come to the knowledge of the party who had appropriated the bonds, it might be a revelation of the weakness of the case against them. Again, he might apply to a private detective, but if he did so, the case would pass out of his hands.

Luke had this piece of information to start upon. He had been informed that Harding left Mr. Armstrong's employment June 17, 1879, and, as was supposed, at once proceeded West. If he could get hold of a file of some Chicago daily paper for the week succeeding, he might look over the last arrivals, and ascertain at what hotel Harding had stopped. This would be something.

"Where can I examine a file of some Chicago daily paper for 1879, Mr. Lawrence?" he asked of the clerk.

"Right here," answered the clerk. "Mr. Goth, the landlord, has a file of the *Times* for the last ten years."

"Would he let me examine the volume for 1879?" asked Luke, eagerly.

"Certainly. I am busy just now, but this afternoon I will have the papers brought down to the reading-room."

He was as good as his word, and at three o'clock in the afternoon Luke sat down before a formidable pile of papers, and began his task of examination.

He began with the paper bearing date June 19, and examined that and the succeeding papers with great care. At length his search was rewarded. In the paper for June 23 Luke discovered the name of James Harding, and, what was a little singular, he was registered at the Ottawa House.

Luke felt quite exultant at this discovery. It might not lead to anything, to be sure, but still it was an encouragement, and seemed to augur well for his ultimate success.

He went with his discovery to his friend the clerk.

"Were you here in June, 1879, Mr. Lawrence?" he asked.

"Yes. I came here in April of that year."

"Of course, you could hardly be expected to remember a casual guest?"

"I am afraid not. What is his name?"

"James Harding."

"James Harding! Yes, I do remember him, and for a very good reason. He took a very severe cold on the way from New York, and he lay here in the hotel sick for two weeks. He was an elderly man, about fifty-five, I should suppose."

"That answers to the description given me. Do you know where he went to from here?"

"There you have me. I can't give you any information on that point."

Luke began to think that his discovery would lead to nothing.

"Stay, though," said the clerk, after a moment's thought. "I remember picking up a small diary in Mr. Harding's room after he left us. I didn't think it of sufficient value to forward to him, nor indeed did I know exactly where to send."

"Can you show me the diary?" asked Luke, hopefully.

"Yes. I have it upstairs in my chamber. Wait five minutes and I will get it for you."

A little later a small, black-covered diary was put in Luke's hand. He opened it eagerly, and began to examine the items jotted down. It appeared partly to note down daily expenses, but on alternate pages there were occasional memorandums. About the fifteenth of May appeared this sentence: "I have reason to think that my sister, Mrs. Ellen Ransom, is now living in

Franklin, Minnesota. She is probably in poor circumstances, her husband having died in poverty a year since. We two are all that is left of a once large family, and now that I am shortly to retire from business with a modest competence, I feel it will be alike my duty and my pleasure to join her, and do what I can to make her comfortable. She has a boy who must now be about twelve years old."

"Come," said Luke, triumphantly, "I am making progress decidedly. My first step will be to go to Franklin, Minnesota, and look up Mr. Harding and his sister. After all, I ought to be grateful to Mr. Coleman, notwithstanding his attempt to rob me. But for him I should never have come to the Ottawa House, and thus I should have lost an important clue."

Luke sat down immediately and wrote to Mr. Armstrong, detailing the discovery he had made—a letter which pleased his employer, and led him to conclude that he had made a good choice in selecting Luke for this confidential mission.

The next day Luke left Chicago and journeyed by the most direct route to Franklin, Minnesota. He ascertained that it was forty miles distant from St. Paul, a few miles off the railroad. The last part of the journey was performed in a stage, and was somewhat wearisome. He breathed a sigh of relief when the stage stopped before the door of a two-story inn with a swinging sign, bearing the name Franklin House.

Luke entered his name on the register and secured a room. He decided to postpone questions till he had enjoyed a good supper and felt refreshed. Then he went out to the desk and opened a conversation with the landlord, or rather submitted first to answering a series of questions propounded by that gentleman.

"You're rather young to be travelin' alone, my young friend," said the innkeeper.

"Yes, sir."

"Where might you be from?"

"From New York."

"Then you're a long way from home. Travelin' for your health?"

"No," answered Luke, with a smile. "I have no trouble with my health."

"You do look pretty rugged, that's a fact. Goin' to settle down in our State?"

"I think not."

"I reckon you're not travelin' on business? You're too young for a drummer."

"The fact is, I am in search of a family that I have been told lives, or used to live, in Franklin."

"What's the name?"

"The lady is a Mrs. Ransom. I wish to see her brother-in-law, Mr. James Harding."

"Sho! You'll have to go farther to find them."

"Don't they live here now?" asked Luke, disappointed.

"No; they moved away six months ago."

"Do you know where they went?" asked Luke, eagerly.

"Not exactly. You see, there was a great stir about gold being plenty in the Black Hills, and Mr. Harding, though he seemed to be pretty well fixed, thought he wouldn't mind pickin' up a little. He induced his sister to go with him—that is, her boy wanted to go, and so she, not wantin' to be left alone, concluded to go, too."

"So they went to the Black Hills. Do you think it would be hard to find them?"

"No; James Harding is a man that's likely to be known wherever he is. Just go to where the miners are thickest, and I allow you'll find him."

Luke made inquiries, and ascertaining the best way of reaching the Black Hills, started the next day.

"If I don't find James Harding, it's because I can't," he said to himself resolutely.

CHAPTER XXXI

TONY DENTON'S CALL

LEAVING Luke on his way to the Black Hills, we will go back to Groveton, to see how matters are moving on there.

Tony Denton had now the excuse he sought for calling upon Prince Duncan. Ostensibly, his errand related to the debt which Randolph had incurred at his saloon, but really he had something more important to speak of. It may be remarked that Squire Duncan, who had a high idea of his own personal importance, looked upon Denton as a low and insignificant person, and never noticed him when they met casually in the street. It is difficult to play the part of an aristocrat in a country village, but that is the rôle which Prince Duncan assumed. Had he been a prince in reality, as he was by name, he could not have borne himself more loftily when he came face to face with those whom he considered his inferiors.

When, in answer to the bell, the servant at Squire Duncan's found Tony Denton standing on the doorstep, she looked at him in surprise.

"Is the squire at home?" asked the saloon keeper.

"I believe so," said the girl, doubtfully.

"I would like to see him. Say Mr. Denton wishes to see him on important business."

The message was delivered.

"Mr. Denton!" repeated the squire, in surprise. "Is it Tony Denton?"

"Yes, sir."

"What can he wish to see me about?"

"He says it's business of importance, sir."

"Well, bring him in."

Prince Duncan assumed his most important attitude and bearing when his visitor entered his presence.

"Mr.—ahem!—Denton, I believe?" he said, as if he found difficulty in recognizing Tony.

"The same."

"I am—ahem!—surprised to hear that you have any business with me."

"Yet so it is, Squire Duncan," said Tony, not perceptibly overawed by the squire's grand manner.

"Elucidate it!" said Prince Duncan, stiffly.

"You may not be aware, Squire Duncan, that your son Randolph has for some time frequented my billiard saloon and has run up a sum of twenty-seven dollars."

"I was certainly not aware of it. Had I been, I should have forbidden his going there. It is no proper place for my son to frequent."

"Well, I don't know about that. It's respectable enough, I guess. At any rate, he seemed to like it, and at his request, for he was not always provided with money, I trusted him till his bill comes to twenty-seven dollars——"

"You surely don't expect me to pay it!" said the squire, coldly. "He is a minor, as you very well know, and when you trusted him you knew you couldn't legally collect your claim."

"Well, squire, I thought I'd take my chances," said Tony, carelessly. "I didn't think you'd be willing to have him owing bills around the village. You're a gentleman, and I was sure you'd settle the debt."

"Then, sir, you made a very great mistake. Such bills as that I do not feel called upon to pay. Was it all incurred for billiards?"

"No; a part of it was for drinks."

"Worse and worse! How can you have the face to come here, Mr. Denton, and tell me that?"

"I don't think it needs any face, squire. It's an honest debt."

"You deliberately entrapped my son, and lured him into your saloon, where he met low companions, and squandered his money and time in drinking and low amusements."

"Come, squire, you're a little too fast. Billiards ain't low. Did you ever see Schaefer and Vignaux play?"

"No, sir; I take no interest in the game. In coming here you have simply wasted your time. You will get no money from me."

"Then you won't pay your son's debt?" asked Tony Denton.

"No."

Instead of rising to go, Tony Denton kept his seat. He regarded Squire Duncan attentively.

"I am sorry, sir," said Prince Duncan, impatiently. "I shall have to cut short this interview."

"I will detain you only five minutes, sir. Have you ascertained who robbed the bank?"

"I have no time for gossip. No, sir."

"I suppose you would welcome any information on the subject?"

Duncan looked at his visitor now with sharp attention.

"Do you know anything about it?" he asked.

"Well, perhaps I do."

"Were you implicated in it?" was the next question.

Tony Denton smiled a peculiar smile.

"No, I wasn't," he answered. "If I had been, I don't think I should have called upon you about the matter. But—I think I know who robbed the bank."

"Who, then?" demanded the squire, with an uneasy look.

Tony Denton rose from his chair, advanced to the door, which was a little ajar, and closed it. Then he resumed.

"One night late—it was after midnight—I was taking a walk,

having just closed my saloon, when it happened that my steps led by the bank. It was dark—not a soul probably in the village was awake save myself, when I saw the door of the bank open and a muffled figure came out with a tin box under his arm. I came closer, yet unobserved, and peered at the person. I recognized him."

"You recognized him?" repeated the squire, mechanically, his face pale and drawn.

"Yes; do you want to know who it was?"

Prince Duncan stared at him, but did not utter a word.

"It was you, the president of the bank!" continued Denton.

"Nonsense, man!" said Duncan, trying to regain his self-control.

"It is not nonsense. I can swear to it."

"I mean that it is nonsense about the robbery. I visited the bank to withdraw a box of my own."

"Of course you can make that statement before the court?" said Tony Denton, coolly.

"But—but—you won't think of mentioning this circumstance?" muttered the squire.

"Will you pay Randolph's bill?"

"Yes—yes; I'll draw a check at once."

"So far, so good; but it isn't far enough. I want more."

"You want more?" ejaculated the squire.

"Yes; I want a thousand-dollar government bond. It's cheap enough for such a secret."

"But I haven't any bonds."

"You can find me one," said Tony, emphatically, "or I'll tell what I know to the directors. You see, I know more than that."

"What do you know?" asked Duncan, terrified.

"I know that you disposed of a part of the bonds on Wall Street, to Sharp & Ketchum. I stood outside when you were up in their office."

Great beads of perspiration gathered upon the banker's brow. This blow was wholly unexpected, and he was wholly unprepared for it. He made a feeble resistance, but in the end, when Tony Denton left the house he had a thousand-dollar bond carefully stowed away in an inside pocket, and Squire Duncan was in such a state of mental collapse that he left his supper untasted.

Randolph was very much surprised when he learned that his father had paid his bill at the billiard saloon, and still more surprised that the squire made very little fuss about it.

CHAPTER XXXII

ON THE WAY TO THE BLACK HILLS

JUST before Luke started for the Black Hills, he received the following letter from his faithful friend Linton. It was sent to New York to the care of Mr. Reed, and forwarded, it not being considered prudent to have it known at Groveton where he was.

"Dear Luke," the letter commenced, "it seems a long time since I have seen you, and I can truly say that I miss you more than I would any other boy in Groveton. I wonder where you are—your mother does not seem to know. She only knows you are traveling for Mr. Reed.

"There is not much news. Groveton, you know, is a quiet place. I see Randolph every day. He seems very curious to know where you are. I think he is disturbed because you have found employment elsewhere. He professes to think that you are selling newspapers in New York, or tending a peanut stand, adding kindly that it is all you are fit for. I have heard a rumor that he was often to be seen playing billiards at Tony Denton's, but I don't know whether it is true. I sometimes think it would do him good to become a poor boy and have to work for a living.

"We are going to Orchard Beach next summer, as usual, and in the fall mamma may take me to Europe to stay a year to learn the French language. Won't that be fine? I wish you could go with me, but I am afraid you can't sell papers or peanuts enough —which is it?—to pay expenses. How long are you going to be away? I shall be glad to see you back, and so will Florence Grant, and all your other friends, of whom you have many in Groveton. Write soon to your affectionate friend,

"LINTON."

This letter quite cheered up Luke, who, in his first absence from home, naturally felt a little lonely at times.

"Linny is a true friend," he said. "He is just as well off as Randolph, but never puts on airs. He is as popular as Randolph is unpopular. I wish I could go to Europe with him."

Upon the earlier portions of Luke's journey to the Black Hills we need not dwell. The last hundred or hundred and fifty miles had to be traversed in a stage, and this form of traveling Luke found wearisome, yet not without interest. There was a spice of danger, too, which added excitement, if not pleasure, to the trip. The Black Hills stage had on more than one occasion been stopped by highwaymen and the passengers robbed.

The thought that this might happen proved a source of nervous alarm to some, of excitement to others.

Luke's fellow passengers included a large, portly man, a merchant from some Western city; a clergyman with a white necktie, who was sent out by some missionary society to start a church at the Black Hills; two or three laboring men, of farmerlike appearance, who were probably intending to work in the mines; one or two others, who could not be classified, and a genuine dude, as far as appearance went, a slender-waisted, soft-voiced young man, dressed in the latest style, who spoke with a slight lisp. He hailed from the city of New York, and called himself Mortimer Plantagenet Sprague. As next to himself, Luke was the youngest passenger aboard the stage, and sat beside him, the two became quite intimate. In spite of his affected manners and somewhat feminine deportment, Luke got the idea that Mr. Sprague was not wholly destitute of manly traits, if occasion should call for their display.

One day, as they were making three miles an hour over a poor road, the conversation fell upon stage robbers.

"What would you do, Colonel Braddon," one passenger asked of the Western merchant, "if the stage were stopped by a gang of ruffians?"

"Shoot 'em down like dogs, sir," was the prompt reply. "If passengers were not so cowardly, stages would seldom be robbed."

All the passengers regarded the valiant colonel with admiring respect, and congratulated themselves that they had with them so doughty a champion in case of need.

"For my part," said the missionary, "I am a man of peace, and I must perforce submit to these men of violence, if they took from me the modest allowance furnished by the society for traveling expenses."

"No doubt, sir," said Colonel Braddon. "You are a minister, and men of your profession are not expected to fight. As for my friend Mr. Sprague," and he directed the attention of the company derisively to the New York dude, "he would, no doubt, engage the robbers single-handed."

"I don't know," drawled Mortimer Sprague. "I am afraid I couldn't tackle more than two, don't you know."

There was a roar of laughter, which did not seem to disturb Mr. Sprague. He did not seem to be at all aware that his companions were laughing at him.

"Perhaps, with the help of my friend, Mr. Larkin," he added, "I might be a match for three."

There was another burst of laughter, in which Luke could not help joining.

"I am afraid I could not help you much, Mr. Sprague," he said.

"I think, Mr. Sprague," said Colonel Braddon, "that you and I will have to do the fighting if any attack is made. If our friend the minister had one of his sermons with him, perhaps that would scare away the highwaymen."

"It would not be the first time they have had an effect on godless men," answered the missionary, mildly, and there was another laugh, this time at the colonel's expense.

"What takes you to the Black Hills, my young friend?" asked Colonel Braddon, addressing Luke.

Other passengers awaited Luke's reply with interest. It was unusual to find a boy of sixteen traveling alone in that region.

"I hope to make some money," answered Luke, smiling. "I suppose that is what we are all after."

He didn't think it wise to explain his errand fully.

"Are you going to dig for gold, Mr. Larkin?" asked Mortimer Sprague. "It's awfully dirty, don't you know, and must be dreadfully hard on the back."

"Probably I am more used to hard work than you, Mr. Sprague," answered Luke.

"I never worked in my life," admitted the dude. "I really don't know a shovel from a hoe."

"Then, if I may be permitted to ask," said Colonel Braddon, "what leads you to the Black Hills, Mr. Sprague?"

"I thought I'd better see something of the country, you know. Besides, I had a bet with another feller about whether the hills were weally black, or not. I bet him a dozen bottles of champagne that they were not black, after all."

This statement was received with a round of laughter, which seemed to surprise Mr. Sprague, who gazed with mild wonder at his companions, saying: "Weally, I can't see what you fellers are laughing at. I thought I'd better come myself, because the other feller might be color-blind, don't you know."

Here Mr. Sprague rubbed his hands and looked about him to see if his joke was appreciated.

"It seems to me that the expense of your journey will foot up considerably more than a dozen bottles of champagne," said one of the passengers.

"Weally, I didn't think of that. You've got a great head, old fellow. After all, a feller's got to be somewhere, and, by Jove!—— What's that?"

This ejaculation was produced by the sudden sinking of the two left wheels in the mire in such a manner that the ponderous Colonel Braddon was thrown into Mr. Sprague's lap

"You see, I had to go somewhere," said Braddon, humorously.

"Weally, I hope we sha'n't get mixed," gasped Sprague. "If it's all the same to you, I'd rather sit in your lap."

"Just a little incident of travel, my dear sir," said Braddon, laughing, as he resumed his proper seat.

"I should call it rather a large incident," said Mr. Sprague, recovering his breath.

"I suppose," said Braddon, who seemed rather disposed to chaff his slender traveling companion, "if you like the Black Hills, you may buy one of them."

"I may," answered Mr. Sprague, letting his glance rest calmly on his big companion. "Suppose we buy one together."

Colonel Braddon laughed, but felt that his joke had not been successful.

The conversation languished after awhile. It was such hard work riding in a lumbering coach, over the most detestable roads, that the passengers found it hard to be sociable. But a surprise was in store. The coach made a sudden stop. Two horsemen appeared at the window, and a stern voice said: "We'll trouble you to get out, gentlemen. We'll take charge of what money and valuables you have about you."

CHAPTER XXXIII

TWO UNEXPECTED CHAMPIONS

IT MAY well be imagined that there was a commotion among the passengers when this stern summons was heard. The highwaymen were but two in number, but each was armed with a revolver, ready for instant use.

One by one the passengers descended from the stage, and stood trembling and panic-stricken in the presence of the masked robbers. There seems to be something in a mask which inspires added terror, though it makes the wearers neither stronger nor more effective.

Luke certainly felt startled and uncomfortable, for he felt that he must surrender the money he had with him, and this would be inconvenient, though the loss would not be his, but his employer's.

But, singularly enough, the passenger who seemed most nervous and terrified was the stalwart Colonel Braddon, who had boasted most noisily of what he would do in case the stage were attacked. He nervously felt in his pockets for his money, his face pale and ashen, and said, imploringly: "Spare my life, gentlemen; I will give you all I have."

"All right, old man," said one of the stage robbers, as he took the proffered pocketbook. Haven't you any more money?"

"No; on my honor, gentlemen. It will leave me penniless."

"Hand over your watch."

With a groan, Colonel Braddon handed over a gold stem-winder, of Waltham make.

"Couldn't you leave me the watch, gentlemen?" he said, imploringly. "It was a present to me last Christmas."

"Can't spare it. Make your friends give you another."

Next came the turn of Mortimer Sprague, the young dude.

"Hand over your spondulics, young feller," said the second gentleman of the road.

"Weally, I'm afraid I can't, without a good deal of twouble."

"Oh, curse the trouble; do as I bid, or I'll break your silly head."

"You see, gentlemen, I keep my money in my boots, don't you know."

"Take off your boots, then, and be quick about it."

"I can't; that is, without help. They're awfully tight, don't you know."

"Which boot is your money in?" asked the road agent, impatiently.

"The right boot."

"Hold it up, then, and I'll help you."

The road agent stooped over, not suspecting any danger, and in doing so laid down his revolver.

In a flash Mortimer Sprague electrified not only his assailants, but all the stage passengers, by producing a couple of revolvers, which he pointed at the two road agents, and in a stern voice, wholly unlike the affected tones in which he had hitherto spoken, said: "Get out of here, you ruffians, or I'll fire!"

The startled road agent tried to pick up his revolver, but Sprague instantly put his foot on it, and repeated the command.

The other road agent, who was occupied with the minister, turned to assist his comrade, when he, too, received a check from an unexpected source.

The minister, who was an old man, had a stout staff, which he used to guide him in his steps. He raised it and brought it down with emphasis on the arm which held the revolver, exclaiming: "The sword of the Lord and of Gideon! I smite thee, thou bold, bad man, not in anger, but as an instrument of retribution."

"Well done, reverend doctor!" exclaimed Mortimer Sprague. "Between us we will lay the rascals out!"

Luke, who was close at hand, secured the fallen revolver before the road agent's arm had got over tingling with the paralyzing blow dealt by the minister, who, in spite of his advanced age, possessed a muscular arm.

"Now git, you two!" exclaimed Mortimer Sprague. "Git, if you want to escape with whole bones!"

Never, perhaps, did two road agents look more foolish than these who had suffered such a sudden and humiliating discomfiture from those among the passengers whom they had feared least.

The young dude and the old missionary had done battle for the entire stage-load of passengers, and vanquished the masked robbers, before whom the rest trembled.

"Stop!" said Colonel Braddon, with a sudden thought. "One of the rascals has got my pocketbook!"

"Which one?" asked Mortimer.

The colonel pointed him out.

Instantly the dude fired, and a bullet whistled within a few inches of the road agent's head.

"Drop that pocketbook!" he exclaimed, "or I'll send another messenger for it; that was only a warning!"

With an execration the thoroughly terrified robber threw down the pocketbook, and the relieved owner hastened forward to pick it up.

"I thought I'd fetch him, don't you know," said the dude, relapsing into his soft drawl.

By this time both the road agents were at a safe distance, and the rescued passengers breathed more freely.

"Really, Mr. Sprague," said Colonel Braddon, pompously, "you are entitled to a great deal of credit for your gallant behavior; you did what I proposed to do. Of course, I had to submit to losing my pocketbook, but I was just preparing to draw my revolver when you got the start of me."

"If I'd only known it, colonel," drawled Mr. Sprague, "I'd have left the job for you. Weally, it would have saved me a good deal of trouble. But I think the reverend doctor here is entitled to the thanks of the company. I never knew exactly what the sword of the Lord and of Gideon was before, but I see it means a good, stout stick."

"I was speaking figuratively, my young friend," said the missionary. "I am not sure but I have acted unprofessionally, but when I saw those men of violence despoiling us, I felt the natural man rise within me, and I smote him hip and thigh."

"I thought you hit him on the arm, doctor," said Mr. Sprague.

"Again I spoke figuratively, my young friend. I cannot say I regret yielding to the impulse that moved me. I feel that I have helped to foil the plans of the wicked."

"Doctor," said one of the miners, "you've true grit. When you preach at the Black Hills, count me and my friends among the listeners. We're all willing to help along your new church, for you're one of the right sort."

"My friends, I will gladly accept your kind proposal, but I trust it will not be solely because I have used this arm of flesh in your defense. Mr. Sprague and I have but acted as humble instruments in the hands of a Higher Power."

"Well, gentlemen," said Colonel Braddon, "I think we may as well get into the stage again and resume our journey."

"What shall I do with this revolver?" asked Luke, indicating the one he had picked up.

"Keep it," said the colonel. "You'll make better used of it than the rascal who lost it."

"I've got an extra one here," said Mortimer Sprague, raising the one on which he had put his foot. "I don't need it myself, so I will offer it to the reverend doctor."

The missionary shook his head.

"I should not know how to use it," he said, "nor indeed am I sure that I should feel justified in doing so."

"May I have it, sir?" asked one of the miners.

"Certainly, if you want it," said Mr. Sprague.

"I couldn't afford to buy one; but I see that I shall need one out here."

In five minutes the stage was again on its way, and no further adventures were met with. About the middle of the next day the party arrived at Deadwood.

CHAPTER XXXIV

FENTON'S GULCH

DEADWOOD, at the time of Luke's arrival, looked more like a mining camp than a town. The first settlers had neither the time nor the money to build elaborate dwellings. Anything, however rough, that would provide a shelter, was deemed sufficient. Luxury was not dreamed of, and even ordinary comforts were only partially supplied. Luke put up at a rude hotel, and the next morning began to make inquiries for Mr. Harding. He ascertained that the person of whom he was in search had arrived not many weeks previous, accompanied by his sister. The latter, however, soon concluded that Deadwood was no suitable residence for ladies, and had returned to her former home, or some place near by. Mr. Harding remained, with a view of trying his luck at the mines.

The next point to be ascertained was to what mines he had directed his steps. This information was hard to obtain. Finally, a man who had just returned to Deadwood, hearing Luke making inquiries of the hotel clerk, said:

"I say, young chap, is the man you are after an old party over fifty, with gray hair and a long nose?"

"I think that is the right description," said Luke, eagerly. "Can you tell me anything about him?"

"The party I mean, he may be Harding, or may be somebody else, is lying sick at Fenton's Gulch, about a day's journey from here—say twenty miles."

"Sick? What is the matter with him?"

"He took a bad cold, and being an old man, couldn't stand it as well as if he were twenty years younger. I left him in an old cabin lying on a blanket, looking about as miserable as you would want to see. Are you a friend of his?"

"I am not acquainted with him," answered Luke, "but I am sent out by a friend of his in the East. I am quite anxious to find him. Can you give me directions?"

"I can do better. I can guide you there. I only came to Deadwood for some supplies, and I go back to-morrow morning."

"If you will let me accompany you I will be very much obliged."

"You can come with me and welcome. I shall be glad of your company. Are you alone?"

"Yes."

"Seems to me you're rather a young chap to come out here alone."

"I suppose I am," returned Luke, smiling, "but there was no one else to come with me. If I find Mr. Harding, I shall be all right."

"I can promise you that. It ain't likely he has got up from his sick-bed and left the mines. I reckon you'll find him flat on his back, as I left him."

Luke learned that his mining friend was known as Jack Baxter. He seemed a sociable and agreeable man, though rather rough in his outward appearance and manners. The next morning they started in company, and were compelled to travel all day. Toward sunset they reached the place known as Fenton's Gulch. It was a wild and dreary-looking place, but had a good reputation for its yield of gold dust.

"That's where you'll find the man you're after," said Baxter, pointing to a dilapidated cabin, somewhat to the left of the mines.

Luke went up to the cabin, the door of which was open, and looked in.

On a pallet in the corner lay a tall man, pale and emaciated. He heard the slight noise at the door, and without turning his head, said: "Come in, friend, whoever you are."

Upon this, Luke advanced into the cabin.

"Is this Mr. James Harding?" he asked.

The sick man turned his head, and his glance rested with surprise upon the boy of sixteen who addressed him.

"Have I seen you before?" he asked.

"No, sir. I have only just arrived at the Gulch. You are Mr. Harding?"

"Yes, that is my name; but how did you know it?"

"I am here in search of you, Mr. Harding."

"How is that?" asked the sick man, quickly. "Is my sister sick?"

"Not that I know of. I come from Mr. Armstrong, in New York."

"You come from Mr. Armstrong?" repeated the sick man, in evident surprise. "Have you any message for me from him?"

"Yes, but that can wait. I am sorry to find you sick. I hope that it is nothing serious."

"It would not be serious if I were in a settlement where I could obtain a good doctor and proper medicines. Everything is serious here. I have no care or attention, and no medicines."

"Do you feel able to get away from here? It would be better for you to be at Deadwood than here."

"If I had anyone to go with me, I might venture to start for Deadwood."

"I am at your service, Mr. Harding."

The sick man looked at Luke with a puzzled expression.

"You are very kind," he said, after a pause. "What is your name?"

"Luke Larkin."

"And you know Mr. Armstrong?"

"Yes. I am his messenger."

"But how came he to send a boy so far? It is not like him."

Luke laughed.

"No doubt you think him unwise," he said. "The fact was, he took me for lack of a better. Besides, the mission was a confidential one, and he thought he could trust me, young as I am."

"You say you have a message for me?" queried Harding.

"Yes!"

"What is it?"

"First, can I do something for your comfort? Can't I get you some breakfast?"

"The message first."

"I will give it at once. Do you remember purchasing some government bonds for Mr. Armstrong a short time before you left his employment?"

"Yes. What of them?"

"Have you preserved the numbers of the bonds?" Luke inquired, anxiously.

"Why do you ask?"

"Because Mr. Armstrong has lost his list, and they have been stolen. Till he learns the numbers, he will stand no chance of identifying or recovering them."

"I am sure I have the numbers. Feel in the pocket of my coat yonder, and you will find a wallet. Take it out and bring it to me."

Luke obeyed directions.

The sick man opened the wallet and began to examine the contents. Finally he drew out a paper, which he unfolded.

"Here is the list. I was sure I had them."

Luke's eyes lighted up with exultation.

It was clear that he had succeeded in his mission. He felt that he had justified the confidence which Mr. Armstrong had reposed in him, and that the outlay would prove not to have been wasted.

"May I copy them?" he asked.

"Certainly, since you are the agent of Mr. Armstrong—or you may have the original paper."

"I will copy them, so that if that paper is lost, I may still have the numbers. And now, what can I do for you?"

The resources of Fenton's Gulch were limited, but Luke succeeded in getting together materials for a breakfast for the sick man. The latter brightened up when he had eaten a sparing meal. It cheered him, also, to find that there was someone to whom he could look for friendly services.

To make my story short, on the second day he felt able to start with Luke for Deadwood, which he reached without any serious effect, except a considerable degree of fatigue.

Arrived at Deadwood, where there were postal facilities, Luke lost no time in writing a letter to Mr. Armstrong, enclosing a list of the stolen bonds. He gave a brief account of the circumstances under which he had found Mr. Harding, and promised to return as soon as he could get the sick man back to his farm in Minnesota.

When this letter was received, Roland Reed was in the merchant's office.

"Look at that, Mr. Reed," said Armstrong, triumphantly. "That boy is as smart as lightning. Some people might have thought me a fool for trusting so young a boy, but the result has justified me. Now my course is clear. With the help of these numbers I shall soon be able to trace the theft and convict the guilty party."

CHAPTER XXXV

BACK IN GROVETON

MEANWHILE, some things occurred in Groveton which require to be chronicled. Since the visit of Tony Denton, and the knowledge that his secret was known, Prince Duncan had changed in manner and appearance. There was an anxious look upon his face, and a haggard look, which led some of his friends to think that his health was affected. Indeed, this was true, for any mental disturbance is likely to affect the body. By way of diverting attention from the cause of this altered appearance, Mr. Duncan began to complain of overwork, and to hint that he might have to travel for his health. It occurred to him privately that circumstances might arise which would make it necessary for him to go to Canada for a lengthened period.

With his secret in the possession of such a man as Tony Denton, he could not feel safe. Besides, he suspected the keeper of the billiard-room would not feel satisfied with the thousand-dollar bond he had extorted from him, but would, after awhile, call for more.

In this he was right.

Scarcely a week had elapsed since his first visit, when the servant announced one morning that a man wished to see him.

"Do you know who it is, Mary?" asked the squire.

"Yes, sir. It's Tony Denton."

Prince Duncan's face contracted, and his heart sank within him. He would gladly have refused to see his visitor, but knowing the hold that Tony had upon him, he did not dare offend him.

"You may tell him to come in," he said, with a troubled look.

"What can the master have to do with a man like that?" thought Mary, wondering. "I wouldn't let him into the house if I was a squire."

Tony Denton entered the room with an assumption of ease which was very disagreeable to Mr. Duncan.

"I thought I'd call to see you, squire," he said.

"Take a seat, Mr. Denton," said the squire coldly.

Tony did not seem at all put out by the coldness of his reception.

"I s'pose you remember what passed at our last meeting, Mr. Duncan," he said, in a jaunty way.

"Well, sir," responded Prince Duncan, in a forbidding tone.

"We came to a little friendly arrangement, if you remember," continued Denton.

"Well, sir, there is no need to refer to the matter now."

"Pardon me, squire, but I am obliged to keep to it."

"Why?"

"Because I've been unlucky."

"I suppose, Mr. Denton," said the squire haughtily, "you are capable of managing your own business. If you don't manage it well, and meet with losses, I certainly am not responsible, and I cannot understand why you bring the matter to me."

"You see, squire," said Tony, with a grin, "I look upon you as a friend, and so it is natural that I should come to you for advice."

"I wish I dared kick the fellow out of the house," thought Prince Duncan. "He is a low scamp, and I don't like the reputation of having such visitors."

Under ordinary circumstances, and but for the secret which Tony possessed, he would not have been suffered to remain in the squire's study five minutes, but conscience makes cowards of us all, and Mr. Duncan felt that he was no longer his own master.

"I'll tell you about the bad luck, squire," Tony resumed. "You know the bond you gave me the last time I called?"

Mr. Duncan winced, and he did not reply.

"I see you remember it. Well, I thought I might have the luck to double it, so I went up to New York, and went to see one of them Wall Street brokers. I asked his advice, and he told me I'd better buy two hundred shares of some kind of stock, leaving the bond with him as margin. He said I was pretty sure to make a good deal of money, and I thought so myself. But the stock went down, and yesterday I got a letter from him, saying that the margin was all exhausted, and I must give him another, or he would sell out the stock."

"Mr. Denton, you have been a fool!" exclaimed Mr. Duncan irritably. "You might have known that would be the result of your insane folly. You've lost your thousand dollars, and what have you got to show for it?"

"You may be right, squire, but I don't want to let the matter end so. I want you to give me another bond."

"You do, eh?" said Duncan indignantly. "So you want to throw away another thousand dollars, do you?"

"If I make good the margin, the stock'll go up likely, and I won't lose anything."

"You can do as you please, of course, but you will have to go elsewhere for your money."

"Will I?" asked Tony coolly. "There is no one else who would let me have the money."

"I won't let you have another cent, you may rely upon that!" exclaimed Prince Duncan furiously.

"I guess you'll think better of that, squire," said Tony, fixing his keen black eyes on the bank president.

"Why should I?" retorted Duncan, but his heart sank within him, for he understood very well what the answer would be.

"Because you know what the consequences of refusal would be," Denton answered coolly.

"I don't understand you," stammered the squire, but it was evident from his startled look that he did.

"I thought you would," returned Tony Denton quietly. "You know very well that my evidence would convict you, as the person who robbed the bank."

"Hush!" ejaculated Prince Duncan, in nervous alarm.

Tony Denton smiled with a consciousness of power.

"I have no wish to expose you," he said, "if you will stand my friend."

In that moment Prince Duncan bitterly regretted the false step he had taken. To be in the power of such a man was, indeed, a terrible form of retribution.

"Explain your meaning," he said reluctantly.

"I want another government bond for a thousand dollars."

"But when I gave you the first, you promised to preserve silence, and trouble me no more."

"I have been unfortunate, as I already explained to you."

"I don't see how that alters matters. You took the risk voluntarily. Why should I suffer because you were imprudent and lost your money?"

"I can't argue with you, squire," said Tony, with an insolent smile. "You are too smart for me. All I have to say is, that I must have another bond."

"Suppose I should give it to you—what assurance have I that you will not make another demand?"

"I will give you the promise in writing, if you like."

"Knowing that I could not make use of any such paper without betraying myself."

"Well, there is that objection, certainly, but I can't do anything better."

"What do you propose to do with the bond?"

"Deposit it with my broker, as I have already told you."

"I advise you not to do so. Make up your mind to lose the first, and keep the second in your own hands."

"I will consider your advice, squire."

But it was very clear that Tony Denton would not follow it.

All at once Prince Duncan brightened up. He had a happy thought. Should it be discovered that the bonds used by Tony Denton belonged to the contents of the stolen box, might he not succeed in throwing the whole blame on the billiard-saloon keeper, and have him arrested as the thief? The possession and use of the bonds would be very damaging, and Tony's reputation was not such as to protect him. Here seemed to be a rift in the clouds—and it was with comparative cheerfulness that Mr. Duncan placed the second bond in the hands of the visitor.

"Of course," he said, "it will be for your interest not to let any one know from whom you obtained this."

"All right. I understand. Well, good morning, squire; I'm glad things are satisfactory."

"Good morning, Mr. Denton."

When Tony had left the room, Prince Duncan threw himself back in his chair and reflected. His thoughts were busy with the man who had just left him, and he tried to arrange some method of throwing the guilt upon Denton. Yet, perhaps, even that would not be necessary. So far as Mr. Duncan knew, there was no record in Mr. Armstrong's possession of the numbers of the bonds, and in that case they would not be identified.

"If I only knew positively that the numbers would not turn up, I should feel perfectly secure, and could realize on the bonds at any time," he thought. "I will wait awhile, and I may see my way clear."

CHAPTER XXXVI

A LETTER FROM LUKE

"THERE'S a letter for you, Linton," said Henry Wagner, as he met Linton Tomkins near the hotel. "I just saw your name on the list."

In the Groveton post-office, as in many country offices, it was the custom to post a list of those for whom letters had been received.

"It must be from Luke," thought Linton, joyfully, and he bent his steps immediately toward the office. No one in the village, outside of Luke's family, missed him more than Linton. Though Luke was two years and a half older, they had always been intimate friends. Linton's family occupied a higher social position, but there was nothing snobbish about Linton, as there was about Randolph, and it made no difference to him that Luke lived in a small and humble cottage, and, till recently, had been obliged to wear old and shabby clothes. In this democratic spirit, Linton was encouraged by his parents, who, while appreciating the refinement which is apt to be connected with liberal means, were too sensible to undervalue sterling merit and good character.

Linton was right. His letter was from Luke. It read thus:

"DEAR LINNY: I was very glad to receive your letter. It made me homesick for a short time. At any rate, it made me wish that I could be back for an hour in dear old Groveton. I cannot tell you where I am, for that is a secret of my employer. I am a long way from home; I can tell you that much. When I get home, I shall be able to tell you all. You will be glad to know that I have succeeded in the mission on which I was sent, and have received a telegram of thanks from my employer.

"It will not be long now before I am back in Groveton. I wonder if my dear friend Randolph will be glad to see me? You can remember me to him when you see him. It will gratify him to know that I am well and doing well, and that my prospects for the future are excellent.

"Give my regards to your father and mother, who have always been kind to me. I shall come and see you the first thing after I return. If you only knew how hard I find it to refrain from telling you all, where I am and what adventures I have met with, how I came near being robbed twice, and many other things, you would appreciate my self-denial. But you shall know all very soon. I have had a good time—the best time in my life. Let mother read this letter, and believe me, dear Lin,

"Your affectionate friend,

"LUKE LARKIN."

Linton's curiosity was naturally excited by the references in Luke's letter.

"Where can Luke be?" he asked. "I wish he were at liberty to tell."

Linton never dreamed, however, that his friend was two thousand miles away, in the wild West. It would have seemed to him utterly improbable.

He was folding up the letter as he was walking homeward, when he met Randolph Duncan.

"What's that, Linton?" he asked. "A love-letter?"

"Not much; I haven't got so far along. It is a letter from Luke Larkin."

"Oh!" sneered Randolph. "I congratulate you on your correspondent. Is he in New York?"

"The letter is postmarked in New York, but he is traveling."

"Traveling? Where is he traveling?"

"He doesn't say. This letter is forwarded by Mr. Reed."

"The man who robbed the bank?"

"What makes you say that? What proof have you that he robbed the bank?"

"I can't prove it, but my father thinks he is the robber. There was something very supicious about that tin box which he handed to Luke."

"It was opened in court, and proved to contain private papers."

"Oh, that's easily seen through. He took out the bonds, and put in the papers. I suppose he has experience in that sort of thing."

"Does your father think that?"

"Yes, he does. What does Luke say?"

"Wait a minute, and I will read you a paragraph," said Linton, with a mischievous smile. Thereupon he read the paragraph in which Randolph was mentioned.

"What does he mean by calling me his dear friend?" exclaimed Randolph indignantly. "I never was his dear friend, and never want to be."

"I believe you, Randolph. Shall I tell you what he means?"

"Yes."

"He means it for a joke. He knows you don't like him, and he isn't breaking his heart over it."

"It's pretty cheeky in him! Just tell him when you write that he needn't call me his dear friend again."

"You might hurt his feelings," said Linton, gravely.

"That for his feelings!" said Randolph, with a snap of his fingers. "You say he's traveling. Shall I tell you what I think he is doing?"

"If you like."

"I think he is traveling with a blacking-box in his hand. It's just the business for him."

"I don't think you are right. He wouldn't make enough in that way to pay traveling expenses. He says he has twice come near being robbed."

Randolph laughed derisively.

"A thief wouldn't make much robbing him," he said. "If he got twenty-five cents he'd be lucky."

"You forget that he has a nice silver watch?"

Randolph frowned. This with him was a sore reflection. Much as he was disposed to look down upon Luke, he was aware that Luke's watch was better than his, and, though he had importuned his father more than once to buy him a gold watch, he saw no immediate prospect of his wish being granted.

"Oh, well, I've talked enough of Luke Larkin," he said, snappishly. "He isn't worth so many words. I am very much surprised that a gentleman's son like you, Linton, should demean himself by keeping company with such a boy."

"There is no boy in the village whom I would rather associate with," said Linton, with sturdy friendship.

"I don't admire your taste, then," said Randolph. "I don't believe your father and mother like you to keep such company."

"There you are mistaken," said Linton, with spirit. "They have an excellent opinion of Luke, and if he should ever need a friend, I am sure my father would be willing to help him."

"Well, I must be going," said Randolph, by no means pleased with this advocacy of Luke. "Come round and see me soon. You never come to our house."

Linton answered politely, but did not mean to become intimate with Randolph, who was by no means to his taste. He knew that it was only his social position that won him the invitation, and that if his father should suddenly lose his property, Randolph's cordiality would be sensibly diminished. Such friendship, he felt, was not to be valued.

"What are you thinking about? You seem in a brown study," said a pleasant voice.

Looking up, Linton recognized his teacher, Mr. Hooper.

"I was thinking of Luke Larkin," answered Linton.

"By the by, where is Luke? I have not seen him for some time."

"He is traveling for Mr. Reed, I believe."

"The man who committed the tin box to his care?"

"Yes, sir."

"Do you know where he is?"

"No, sir. I have just received a letter from him, but he says he is not at liberty to mention where he is."

"Will he be home soon?"

"Yes, I think so."

"I shall be glad to see him. He is one of the most promising of my pupils."

Linton's expressive face showed the pleasure he felt at this commendation of his friend. He felt more gratified than if Mr. Hooper had directly praised him.

"Luke can stand Randolph's depreciation," he reflected, "with such a friend as Mr. Hooper."

Linton was destined to meet plenty of acquaintances. Scarcely had he parted from Mr. Hooper, when Tony Denton met him. The keeper of the billiard-room was always on the alert to ingratiate himself with the young people of the village, looking upon them as possible patrons of his rooms. He would have been glad to draw in Linton, on account of his father's prominent position in the village.

"Good day, my young friend," he said, with suavity.

"Good day, Mr. Denton," responded Linton, who thought it due to himself to be polite, though he did not fancy Mr. Denton.

"I should be very glad to have you look in at my billiard-room, Mr. Linton," continued Tony.

"Thank you sir, but I don't think my father would like to have me visit a billiard-saloon—at any rate, till I am older."

"Oh, I'll see that you come to no harm. If you don't want to play, you can look on."

"At any rate, I am obliged to you for your polite invitation."

"Oh, I like to have the nice boys of the village around me. Your friend Randolph Duncan often visits me."

"So I have heard," replied Linton.

"Well, I won't keep you, but remember my invitation."

"I am not very likely to accept," thought Linton. "I have heard that Randolph visits the billiard-room too often for his good."

CHAPTER XXXVII

AN INCIDENT ON THE CARS

AS SOON as possible, Luke started on his return to New York. He had enjoyed his journey, but now he felt a longing to see home and friends once more. His journey to Chicago was uneventful. He stayed there a few hours, and then started on his way home. On his trip from Chicago to Detroit he fell in with an old acquaintance unexpectedly.

When about thirty miles from Detroit, having as a seatmate a very large man, who compressed him within uncomfortable limits, he took his satchel, and passing into the car next forward, took a seat a few feet from the door. He had scarcely seated himself when, looking around, he discovered, in the second seat beyond, his old Chicago acquaintance, Mr. J. Madison Coleman. He was as smooth and affable as ever, and was chatting pleasantly with a rough, farmerlike-looking man, who seemed very much taken with his attractive companion.

"I wonder what mischief Coleman is up to now?" thought Luke.

He was so near that he was able to hear the conversation that passed between them.

"Yes, my friend," said Mr. Coleman, "I am well acquainted with Detroit. Business has called me there very often, and it will give me great pleasure to be of service to you in any way."

"What business are you in?" inquired the other.

"I am traveling for H. B. Claflin & Co., of New York. Of course you have heard of them. They are the largest wholesale dry-goods firm in the United States."

"You don't say so!" returned the farmer respectfully. "Do you get pretty good pay?"

"I am not at liberty to tell just what pay I get," said Mr. Coleman, "but I am willing to admit that it is over four thousand dollars."

"You don't say so!" ejaculated the farmer. "My! I think myself pretty lucky when I make a thousand dollars a year."

"Oh, well, my dear sir, your expenses are very light compared to mine. I spend about ten dollars a day on an average."

"Jehu!" ejaculated the farmer. "Well, that is a pile. Do all the men that travel for your firm get as much salary as you?"

"Oh, no; I am one of the principal salesmen, and am paid extra. I am always successful, if I do say it myself, and the firm know it, and pay me accordingly. They know that several other firms are after me, and would get me away if they didn't pay me my price."

"I suppose you know all about investments, being a business man?"

"Yes, I know a great deal about them," answered Mr. Coleman, his eyes sparkling with pleasure at this evidence that his companion had money. "If you have any money to invest, I shall be very glad to advise you."

"Well, you see, I've just had a note for two hundred and fifty dollars paid in by a neighbor who's been owin' it for two years, and I thought I'd go up to Detroit and put it in the savings-bank."

"My good friend, the savings-bank pays but a small rate of interest. I think I know a business man of Detroit who will take your money and pay you ten per cent."

"Ten per cent.!" exclaimed the farmer joyfully. "My! I didn't think I could get over four or six."

"So you can't, in a general way," answered Coleman. "But business men, who are turning over their money once a month, can afford to pay a good deal more."

"But is your friend safe?" he inquired, anxiously.

"Safe as the Bank of England," answered Coleman. "I've lent him a thousand dollars at a time, myself, and always got principal and interest regularly. I generally have a few thousand invested," he added, in a matter-of-course manner.

"I'd be glad to get ten per cent.," said the farmer. "That would be twenty-five dollars a year on my money."

"Exactly. I dare say you didn't get over six per cent. on the note."

"I got seven, but I had to wait for the interest sometimes."

"You'll never have to wait for interest if you lend to my friend. I am only afraid he won't be willing to take so small a sum. Still, I'll speak a good word for you, and he will make an exception in your favor."

"Thank you, sir," said the farmer gratefully. "I guess I'll let him have it."

"You couldn't do better. He's a high-minded, responsible man. I would offer to take the money myself, but I really have no use for it. I have at present two thousand dollars in bank waiting for investment."

"You don't say so!" said the farmer, eying Coleman with the respect due to so large a capitalist.

"Yes, I've got it in the savings-bank for the time being. If my friend can make use of it, I shall let him have it. He's just as safe as a savings-bank."

The farmer's confidence in Mr. Coleman was evidently fully established. The young man talked so smoothly and confidently that he would have imposed upon one who had seen far more of the world than Farmer Jones.

"I'm in luck to fall in with you, Mr.——"

"Coleman," said the drummer, with suavity. "J. Madison Coleman. My grandfather was a cousin of President James Madison, and that accounts for my receiving that name."

The farmer's respect was further increased. It was quite an event to fall in with so near a relative of an illustrious ex-President, and he was flattered to find that a young man of such lineage was disposed to treat him with such friendly familiarity.

"Are you going to stay long in Detroit?" asked the farmer.

"Two or three days. I shall be extremely busy, but I shall find time to attend to your business. In fact, I feel an interest in you, my friend, and shall be glad to do you a service."

"You are very kind, and I'm obleeged to you," said the farmer gratefully.

"Now, if you will excuse me for a few minutes, I will go into the smoking-car and have a smoke."

When he had left the car, Luke immediately left his seat, and went forward to where the farmer was sitting.

"Excuse me," he said, "but I saw you talking to a young man just now."

"Yes," answered the farmer complacently, "he's a relative of President Madison."

"I want to warn you against him. I know him to be a swindler."

"What!" exclaimed the farmer, eying Luke suspiciously. "Who be you? You're nothing but a boy."

"That is true, but I am traveling on business. This Mr. Coleman tried to rob me about a fortnight since, and nearly succeeded. I heard him talking to you about money."

"Yes, he was going to help me invest some money I have with me. He said he could get me ten per cent."

"Take my advice, and put it in a savings bank. Then it will be safe. No man who offers to pay ten per cent. for money can be relied upon."

"Perhaps you want to rob me yourself?" said the farmer suspiciously.

"Do I look like it?" asked Luke, smiling. "Isn't my advice good, to put the money in a savings-bank? But I will tell you how I fell in with Mr. Coleman, and how he tried to swindle me, and then you can judge for yourself."

This Luke did briefly, and his tone and manner carried conviction. The farmer became extremely indignant at the intended fraud, and promised to have nothing to do with Coleman.

"I will take my old seat, then," said Luke. "I don't want Coleman to know who warned you."

Presently, Coleman came back and was about to resume his seat beside the farmer.

"You see I have come back," he said.

"You needn't have troubled yourself," said the farmer, with a lowering frown. "You nearly took me in with your smooth words, but I've got my money yet, and I mean to keep it. Your friend can't have it."

"What does all this mean, my friend?" asked Coleman, in real amazement. "Is it possible you distrust me? Why, I was going to put myself to inconvenience to do you a service."

"Then you needn't. I know you. You wanted to swindle me out of my two hundred and fifty dollars."

"Sir, you insult me!" exclaimed Coleman, with lofty indignation. "What do I—a rich man—want of your paltry two hundred and fifty dollars?"

"I don't believe you are a rich man. Didn't I tell you, I have been warned against you?"

"Who dared to talk against me?" asked Coleman indignantly. Then, casting his eyes about, he noticed Luke for the first time. Now it was all clear to him.

Striding up to Luke's seat, he said threateningly, "Have you been talking against me, you young jackanapes?"

"Yes, Mr. Coleman, I have," answered Luke steadily. "I thought it my duty to inform this man of your character. I have advised him to put his money into a savings-bank."

"Curse you for an impertinent meddler!" said Coleman wrathfully. "I'll get even with you for this!"

"You can do as you please," said Luke calmly.

Coleman went up to the farmer and said, abruptly, "You've been imposed upon by an unprincipled boy. He's been telling you lies about me."

"He has given me good advice," said the farmer sturdily, "and I shall follow it."

"You are making a fool of yourself!"

"That is better than to be made fool of, and lose my money."

Coleman saw that the game was lost, and left the car. He would gladly have assaulted Luke, but knew that it would only get him into trouble.

CHAPTER XXXVIII

LUKE'S RETURN

MR. ARMSTRONG was sitting in his office one morning when the door opened, and Luke entered, his face flushed with health, and his cheeks browned by exposure.

"You see I've got back, Mr. Armstrong," he said, advancing with a smile.

"Welcome home, Luke!" exclaimed the merchant heartily, grasping our hero's hand cordially.

"I hope you are satisfied with me," said Luke.

"Satisfied! I ought to be. You have done yourself the greatest credit. It is seldom a boy of your age exhibits such good judgment and discretion."

"Thank you, sir," said Luke gratefully. "I was obliged to spend a good deal of money," he added, "and I have arrived in New York with only three dollars and seventy-five cents in my pocket."

"I have no fault to find with your expenses," said Mr. Armstrong promptly. "Nor would I have complained if you had spent twice as much. The main thing was to succeed, and you have succeeded."

"I am glad to hear you speak so," said Luke, relieved. "To me it seemed a great deal of money. You gave me two hundred dollars, and I have less than five dollars left. Here it is!" and Luke drew the sum from his pocket, and tendered it to the merchant.

"I can't take it," said Mr. Armstrong. "You don't owe me any money. It is I who am owing you. Take this on account," and he drew a roll of bills from his pocketbook and handed it to Luke. "Here are a hundred dollars on account," he continued.

"This is too much, Mr. Armstrong," said Luke, quite overwhelmed with the magnitude of the gift.

"Let me be the judge of that," said Mr. Armstrong kindly. "There is only one thing, Luke, that I should have liked to have you do."

"What is that, sir?"

"I should like to have had you bring me a list of the numbers certified to by Mr. Harding."

Luke's answer was to draw from the inside pocket of his vest a paper signed by the old bookkeeper, containing a list of the numbers, regularly subscribed and certified to.

"Is that what you wished, sir?" he asked.

"You are a wonderful boy," said the merchant admiringly. "Was this your idea, or Mr. Harding's?"

"I believe I suggested it to him," said Luke modestly.

"That makes all clear sailing," said Mr. Armstrong. "Here are fifty dollars more. You deserve it for your thoughtfulness."

"You have given me enough already," said Luke, drawing back.

"My dear boy, it is evident that you still have something to learn in the way of business. When a rich old fellow offers you money, which he can well afford, you had better take it."

"That removes all my objections," said Luke. "But I am afraid you will spoil me with your liberality, Mr. Armstrong."

"I will take the risk of it. But here is another of your friends."

The door had just opened, and Roland Reed entered. There was another cordial greeting, and Luke felt that it was pleasant, indeed, to have two such good friends.

"When are you going to Groveton, Luke?" asked Mr. Reed.

"I shall go this afternoon, if there is nothing more you wish me to do. I am anxious to see my mother."

"That is quite right, Luke. Your mother is your best friend, and deserves all the attention you can give her. I shall probably go to Groveton myself to-morrow."

After Luke had left the office, Mr. Reed remained to consult with the merchant as to what was the best thing to do. Both were satisfied that Prince Duncan, the president of the bank, was the real thief who had robbed the bank. There were two courses open—a criminal prosecution, or a private arrangement which should include the return of the stolen property. The latter course was determined upon, but should it prove ineffective, severer measures were to be resorted to.

CHAPTER XXXIX

HOW LUKE WAS RECEIVED

LUKE'S return to Groveton was received with delight by his mother and his true friend Linton. Naturally Randolph displayed the same feelings toward him as ever. It so chanced that he met Luke only an hour after his arrival. He would have passed him by unnoticed but for the curiosity he felt to know where he had been, and what he was intending to do.

"Humph! so you're back again!" he remarked.

"Yes," answered Luke, with a smile. "I hope you haven't missed me much, Randolph."

"Oh, I've managed to live through it," returned Randolph, with what he thought to be cutting sarcasm.

"I am glad of that."

"Where were you?" asked Randolph, abruptly.

"I was in New York a part of the time," said Luke.

"Where were you the rest of the time?"

"I was traveling."

"That sounds large. Perhaps you were traveling with a hand-organ."

"Perhaps I was."

"Well, what are you going to do now?"

"Thank you for your kind interest in me, Randolph. I will tell you as soon as I know."

"Oh, you needn't think I feel interest in you."

"Then I won't."

"You are impertinent," said Randolph, scowling. It dawned upon him that Luke was chaffing him.

"I don't mean to be. If I have been, I apologize. If you know of any situation which will pay me a fair sum, I wish you would mention me."

"I'll see about it," said Randolph, in an important tone. He was pleased at Luke's change of tone. "I don't think you can get back as janitor, for my father doesn't like you."

"Couldn't you intercede for me, Randolph?"

"Why, the fact is, you put on so many airs, for a poor boy,

that I shouldn't feel justified in recommending you. It is your own fault."

"Well, perhaps it is," said Luke.

"I am glad you acknowledge it. I don't know but my father will give you a chance to work round our house, make fires, and run errands."

"What would he pay?" asked Luke, in a businesslike tone.

"He might pay a dollar and a half a week."

"I'm afraid I couldn't support myself on that."

"Oh, well, that's your lookout. It's better than loafing round doing nothing."

"You're right there, Randolph."

"I'll just mention it to father, then."

"No, thank you. I shouldn't wonder if Mr. Reed might find something for me to do."

"Oh, the man that robbed the bank?" said Randolph, turning up his nose.

"It may soon be discovered that some one else robbed the bank."

"I don't believe it."

Here the two boys parted.

"Luke," said Linton, the same day, "have you decided what you are going to do?"

"Not yet; but I have friends who, I think, will look out for me."

"Because my father says he will find you a place if you fail to get one elsewhere."

"Tell your father that I think he is very kind. There is no one to whom I would more willingly be indebted for a favor. If I should find myself unemployed, I will come to him."

"All right! I am going to drive over to Coleraine"—the next town—"this afternoon. Will you go with me?"

"I should like nothing better."

"What a difference there is between Randolph and Linton!" thought Luke.

CHAPTER XL

THE BANK ROBBER IS FOUND

TONY DENTON lost no time in going up to the city with the second bond he had extracted from the fears of Prince Duncan. He went directly to the office of his brokers, Gay & Sears, and announced that he was prepared to deposit additional margin.

The bond was received, and taken to the partners in the back office. Some four minutes elapsed, and the clerk reappeared.

"Mr. Denton, will you step into the back office?" he said.

"Certainly," answered Tony cheerfully.

He found the two brokers within.

"This is Mr. Denton?" said the senior partner.

"Yes, sir."

"You offer this bond as additional margin on the shares we hold in your name?"

"Yes, of course."

"Mr. Denton," said Mr. Gay searchingly, "where did you get this bond?"

"Where did I get it?" repeated Denton nervously. "Why, I bought it."

"How long since?"

"About a year."

The two partners exchanged glances.

"Where do you live, Mr. Denton?"

"In Groveton."

"Ahem! Mr. Sears, will you be kind enough to draw out the necessary papers?"

Tony Denton felt relieved. The trouble seemed to be over.

Mr. Gay at the same time stepped into the main office and gave a direction to one of the clerks.

Mr. Sears drew out a large sheet of foolscap, and began, in very deliberate fashion, to write. He kept on writing for some minutes. Tony Denton wondered why so much writing should be necessary in a transaction of this kind. Five minutes later a young man looked into the office, and said, addressing Mr. Gay: "All right!"

Upon that Mr. Sears suspended writing.

"Mr. Denton," said Mr. Gay, "are you aware that this bond

which you have brought us was stolen from the Groveton Bank?"

"I—don't—believe—it," gasped Denton, turning pale.

"The numbers of the stolen bonds have been sent to all the bankers and brokers in the city. This is one, and the one you brought us not long since is another. Do you persist in saying that you bought this bond a year ago?"

"No, no!" exclaimed Denton, terrified.

"Did you rob the bank?"

"No, I didn't!" ejaculated the terrified man, wiping the perspiration from his brow.

"Where, then, did you get the bonds?"

"I got them both from Prince Duncan, president of the bank."

Both partners looked surprised.

One of them went to the door of the office, and called in Mr. Armstrong, who, as well as a policeman, had been sent for.

Tony Denton's statement was repeated to him.

"I am not surprised," he said. "I expected it."

Tony Denton now made a clean breast of the whole affair, and his words were taken down.

"Are you willing to go to Groveton with me, and repeat this in presence of Mr. Duncan?" asked Mr. Armstrong.

"Yes."

"Will you not have him arrested?" asked Mr. Gay.

"No, he has every reason to keep faith with me."

It was rather late in the day when Mr. Armstrong, accompanied by Tony Denton, made their appearance at the house of Prince Duncan. When the banker's eyes rested on the strangely assorted pair, his heart sank within him. He had a suspicion of what it meant.

"We have called on you, Mr. Duncan, on a matter of importance," said Mr. Armstrong.

"Very well," answered Duncan faintly.

"It is useless to mince matters. I have evidence outside of this man's to show that it was you who robbed the bank of which you are president, and appropriated to your own use the bonds which it contained."

"This is a strange charge to bring against a man in my position. Where is your proof?" demanded Duncan, attempting to bluster.

"I have Mr. Denton's evidence that he obtained two thousand-dollar bonds of you."

"Very well, suppose I did sell him two such bonds?"

"They were among the bonds stolen."

"It is not true. They were bonds I have had for five years."

"Your denial is useless. The numbers betray you."

"You did not have the numbers of the bonds."

"So you think, but I have obtained them from an old book-keeper of mine, now at the West. I sent a special messenger out to obtain the list from him. Would you like to know who the messenger was?"

"Who was it?"

"Luke Larkin."

"That boy!" exclaimed Duncan bitterly.

"Yes, that boy supplied me with the necessary proof. And now, I have a word to say; I can send you to prison, but for the sake of your family I would prefer to spare you. But the bonds must be given up."

"I haven't them all in my possession."

"Then you must pay me the market price of those you have used. The last one given to this man is safe."

"It will reduce me to poverty," said Prince Duncan in great agitation.

"Nevertheless, it must be done!" said Mr. Armstrong sternly. "Moreover, you must resign your position as president of the bank, and on that condition you will be allowed to go free, and I will not expose you."

Of course, Squire Duncan was compelled to accept these terms. He saved a small sum out of the wreck of his fortune, and with his family removed to the West, where they were obliged to adopt a very different style of living. Randolph is now an office boy at a salary of four dollars a week, and is no longer able to swagger and boast as he has done hitherto. Mr. Tomkins, Linton's father, was elected president of the Groveton Bank in place of Mr. Duncan, much to the satisfaction of Luke.

Roland Reed, much to the suprise of Luke, revealed himself as a cousin of Mr. Larkin, who for twenty-five years had been lost sight of. He had changed his name, on account of some trouble into which he had been betrayed by Prince Duncan, and thus had not been recognized.

"You need be under no anxiety about Luke and his prospects," he said to Mrs. Larkin. "I shall make over to him ten thousand dollars at once, constituting myself his guardian, and will see that he is well started in business. My friend Mr. Armstrong proposes to take him into his office, if you do not object, at a liberal salary."

"I shall miss him very much," said Mrs. Larkin, "though I am thankful that he is to be so well provided for."

"He can come home every Saturday night, and stay until Monday morning," said Mr. Reed, who, by the way, chose to retain his name in place of his old one. "Will that satisfy you?"

"It ought to, surely, and I am grateful to Providence for all the blessings which it has showered upon me and mine."

There was another change. Mr. Reed built a neat and commodious house in the pleasantest part of the village and there Mrs. Larkin removed with his little daughter, of whom she still had the charge. No one rejoiced more sincerely at Luke's good fortune than Linton, who throughout had been a true and faithful friend. He is at present visiting Europe with his mother, and has written an earnest letter, asking Luke to join him. But Luke feels that he cannot leave a good business position, and must postpone the pleasure of traveling till he is older.

Mr. J. Madison Coleman, the enterprising drummer, has got into trouble, and is at present an inmate of the State penitentiary at Joliet, Illinois. It is fortunate for the traveling public, so many of whom he has swindled, that he is for a time placed where he can do no more mischief.

So closes an eventful passage in the life of Luke Larkin. He has struggled upward from a boyhood of privation and self-denial into a youth and manhood of prosperity and honor. There has been some luck about it, I admit, but after all he is indebted for most of his good fortune to his own good qualities.

THE END

A CATALOG OF SELECTED

DOVER BOOKS

IN ALL FIELDS OF INTEREST

A CATALOG OF SELECTED DOVER BOOKS IN ALL FIELDS OF INTEREST

THE BOOK OF BEASTS: Being a Translation from a Latin Bestiary of the Twelfth Century, T. H. White. Wonderful catalog real and fanciful beasts: manticore, griffin, phoenix, amphivius, jaculus, many more. White's witty erudite commentary on scientific, historical aspects. Fascinating glimpse of medieval mind. Illustrated. 296pp. 5⅜ × 8¼. (Available in U.S. only) 24609-4 Pa. $6.95

FRANK LLOYD WRIGHT: ARCHITECTURE AND NATURE With 160 Illustrations, Donald Hoffmann. Profusely illustrated study of influence of nature—especially prairie—on Wright's designs for Fallingwater, Robie House, Guggenheim Museum, other masterpieces. 96pp. 9¼ × 10¾. 25098-9 Pa. $7.95

FRANK LLOYD WRIGHT'S FALLINGWATER, Donald Hoffmann. Wright's famous waterfall house: planning and construction of organic idea. History of site, owners, Wright's personal involvement. Photographs of various stages of building. Preface by Edgar Kaufmann, Jr. 100 illustrations. 112pp. 9¼ × 10.
23671-4 Pa. $8.95

YEARS WITH FRANK LLOYD WRIGHT: Apprentice to Genius, Edgar Tafel. Insightful memoir by a former apprentice presents a revealing portrait of Wright the man, the inspired teacher, the greatest American architect. 372 black-and-white illustrations. Preface. Index. vi + 228pp. 8¼ × 11. 24801-1 Pa. $10.95

THE STORY OF KING ARTHUR AND HIS KNIGHTS, Howard Pyle. Enchanting version of King Arthur fable has delighted generations with imaginative narratives of exciting adventures and unforgettable illustrations by the author. 41 illustrations. xviii + 313pp. 6⅛ × 9¼. 21445-1 Pa. $6.95

THE GODS OF THE EGYPTIANS, E. A. Wallis Budge. Thorough coverage of numerous gods of ancient Egypt by foremost Egyptologist. Information on evolution of cults, rites and gods; the cult of Osiris; the Book of the Dead and its rites; the sacred animals and birds; Heaven and Hell, and more. 956pp. 6⅛ × 9¼.
22055-9, 22056-7 Pa., Two-vol. set $21.90

A THEOLOGICO-POLITICAL TREATISE, Benedict Spinoza. Also contains unfinished *Political Treatise*. Great classic on religious liberty, theory of government on common consent. R. Elwes translation. Total of 421pp. 5⅜ × 8½.
20249-6 Pa. $6.95

INCIDENTS OF TRAVEL IN CENTRAL AMERICA, CHIAPAS, AND YUCATAN, John L. Stephens. Almost single-handed discovery of Maya culture; exploration of ruined cities, monuments, temples; customs of Indians. 115 drawings. 892pp. 5⅜ × 8½. 22404-X, 22405-8 Pa., Two-vol. set $15.90

LOS CAPRICHOS, Francisco Goya. 80 plates of wild, grotesque monsters and caricatures. Prado manuscript included. 183pp. 6⅝ × 9⅝. 22384-1 Pa. $5.95

AUTOBIOGRAPHY: The Story of My Experiments with Truth, Mohandas K. Gandhi. Not hagiography, but Gandhi in his own words. Boyhood, legal studies, purification, the growth of the Satyagraha (nonviolent protest) movement. Critical, inspiring work of the man who freed India. 480pp. 5⅜ × 8½. (Available in U.S. only)
24593-4 Pa. $6.95

HOW TO WRITE, Gertrude Stein. Gertrude Stein claimed anyone could understand her unconventional writing—here are clues to help. Fascinating improvisations, language experiments, explanations illuminate Stein's craft and the art of writing. Total of 414pp. 4⅜ × 6⅜. 23144-5 Pa. $6.95

ADVENTURES AT SEA IN THE GREAT AGE OF SAIL: Five Firsthand Narratives, edited by Elliot Snow. Rare true accounts of exploration, whaling, shipwreck, fierce natives, trade, shipboard life, more. 33 illustrations. Introduction. 353pp. 5⅜ × 8½. 25177-2 Pa. $8.95

THE HERBAL OR GENERAL HISTORY OF PLANTS, John Gerard. Classic descriptions of about 2,850 plants—with over 2,700 illustrations—includes Latin and English names, physical descriptions, varieties, time and place of growth, more. 2,706 illustrations. xlv + 1,678pp. 8½ × 12¼. 23147-X Cloth. $75.00

DOROTHY AND THE WIZARD IN OZ, L. Frank Baum. Dorothy and the Wizard visit the center of the Earth, where people are vegetables, glass houses grow and Oz characters reappear. Classic sequel to *Wizard of Oz*. 256pp. 5⅜ × 8. 24714-7 Pa. $4.95

SONGS OF EXPERIENCE: Facsimile Reproduction with 26 Plates in Full Color, William Blake. This facsimile of Blake's original "Illuminated Book" reproduces 26 full-color plates from a rare 1826 edition. Includes "The Tyger," "London," "Holy Thursday," and other immortal poems. 26 color plates. Printed text of poems. 48pp. 5¼ × 7. 24636-1 Pa. $3.50

SONGS OF INNOCENCE, William Blake. The first and most popular of Blake's famous "Illuminated Books," in a facsimile edition reproducing all 31 brightly colored plates. Additional printed text of each poem. 64pp. 5¼ × 7. 22764-2 Pa. $3.50

PRECIOUS STONES, Max Bauer. Classic, thorough study of diamonds, rubies, emeralds, garnets, etc.: physical character, occurrence, properties, use, similar topics. 20 plates, 8 in color. 94 figures. 659pp. 6⅛ × 9¼. 21910-0, 21911-9 Pa., Two-vol. set $15.90

ENCYCLOPEDIA OF VICTORIAN NEEDLEWORK, S. F. A. Caulfeild and Blanche Saward. Full, precise descriptions of stitches, techniques for dozens of needlecrafts—most exhaustive reference of its kind. Over 800 figures. Total of 679pp. 8⅛ × 11. Two volumes. Vol. 1 22800-2 Pa. $11.95
Vol. 2 22801-0 Pa. $11.95

THE MARVELOUS LAND OF OZ, L. Frank Baum. Second Oz book, the Scarecrow and Tin Woodman are back with hero named Tip, Oz magic. 136 illustrations. 287pp. 5⅜ × 8½. 20692-0 Pa. $5.95

WILD FOWL DECOYS, Joel Barber. Basic book on the subject, by foremost authority and collector. Reveals history of decoy making and rigging, place in American culture, different kinds of decoys, how to make them, and how to use them. 140 plates. 156pp. 7⅞ × 10¾. 20011-6 Pa. $8.95

HISTORY OF LACE, Mrs. Bury Palliser. Definitive, profusely illustrated chronicle of lace from earliest times to late 19th century. Laces of Italy, Greece, England, France, Belgium, etc. Landmark of needlework scholarship. 266 illustrations. 672pp. 6⅛ × 9¼. 24742-2 Pa. $14.95

ILLUSTRATED GUIDE TO SHAKER FURNITURE, Robert Meader. All furniture and appurtenances, with much on unknown local styles. 235 photos. 146pp. 9 × 12. 22819-3 Pa. $8.95

WHALE SHIPS AND WHALING: A Pictorial Survey, George Francis Dow. Over 200 vintage engravings, drawings, photographs of barks, brigs, cutters, other vessels. Also harpoons, lances, whaling guns, many other artifacts. Comprehensive text by foremost authority. 207 black-and-white illustrations. 288pp. 6 × 9. 24808-9 Pa. $8.95

THE BERTRAMS, Anthony Trollope. Powerful portrayal of blind self-will and thwarted ambition includes one of Trollope's most heartrending love stories. 497pp. 5⅜ × 8½. 25119-5 Pa. $9.95

ADVENTURES WITH A HAND LENS, Richard Headstrom. Clearly written guide to observing and studying flowers and grasses, fish scales, moth and insect wings, egg cases, buds, feathers, seeds, leaf scars, moss, molds, ferns, common crystals, etc.—all with an ordinary, inexpensive magnifying glass. 209 exact line drawings aid in your discoveries. 220pp. 5⅜ × 8½. 23330-8 Pa. $4.95

RODIN ON ART AND ARTISTS, Auguste Rodin. Great sculptor's candid, wide-ranging comments on meaning of art; great artists; relation of sculpture to poetry, painting, music; philosophy of life, more. 76 superb black-and-white illustrations of Rodin's sculpture, drawings and prints. 119pp. 8⅜ × 11¼. 24487-3 Pa. $7.95

FIFTY CLASSIC FRENCH FILMS, 1912–1982: A Pictorial Record, Anthony Slide. Memorable stills from Grand Illusion, Beauty and the Beast, Hiroshima, Mon Amour, many more. Credits, plot synopses, reviews, etc. 160pp. 8¼ × 11. 25256-6 Pa. $11.95

THE PRINCIPLES OF PSYCHOLOGY, William James. Famous long course complete, unabridged. Stream of thought, time perception, memory, experimental methods; great work decades ahead of its time. 94 figures. 1,391pp. 5⅜ × 8½. 20381-6, 20382-4 Pa., Two-vol. set $23.90

BODIES IN A BOOKSHOP, R. T. Campbell. Challenging mystery of blackmail and murder with ingenious plot and superbly drawn characters. In the best tradition of British suspense fiction. 192pp. 5⅜ × 8½. 24720-1 Pa. $3.95

CALLAS: PORTRAIT OF A PRIMA DONNA, George Jellinek. Renowned commentator on the musical scene chronicles incredible career and life of the most controversial, fascinating, influential operatic personality of our time. 64 black-and-white photographs. 416pp. 5⅜ × 8¼. 25047-4 Pa. $8.95

GEOMETRY, RELATIVITY AND THE FOURTH DIMENSION, Rudolph Rucker. Exposition of fourth dimension, concepts of relativity as Flatland characters continue adventures. Popular, easily followed yet accurate, profound. 141 illustrations. 133pp. 5⅜ × 8½. 23400-2 Pa. $3.95

HOUSEHOLD STORIES BY THE BROTHERS GRIMM, with pictures by Walter Crane. 53 classic stories—Rumpelstiltskin, Rapunzel, Hansel and Gretel, the Fisherman and his Wife, Snow White, Tom Thumb, Sleeping Beauty, Cinderella, and so much more—lavishly illustrated with original 19th century drawings. 114 illustrations. x + 269pp. 5⅜ × 8½. 21080-4 Pa. $4.95

SUNDIALS, Albert Waugh. Far and away the best, most thorough coverage of ideas, mathematics concerned, types, construction, adjusting anywhere. Over 100 illustrations. 230pp. 5⅜ × 8½. 22947-5 Pa. $4.95

PICTURE HISTORY OF THE NORMANDIE: With 190 Illustrations, Frank O. Braynard. Full story of legendary French ocean liner: Art Deco interiors, design innovations, furnishings, celebrities, maiden voyage, tragic fire, much more. Extensive text. 144pp. 8⅞ × 11¾. 25257-4 Pa. $10.95

THE FIRST AMERICAN COOKBOOK: A Facsimile of "American Cookery," 1796, Amelia Simmons. Facsimile of the first American-written cookbook published in the United States contains authentic recipes for colonial favorites—pumpkin pudding, winter squash pudding, spruce beer, Indian slapjacks, and more. Introductory Essay and Glossary of colonial cooking terms. 80pp. 5⅜ × 8½. 24710-4 Pa. $3.50

101 PUZZLES IN THOUGHT AND LOGIC, C. R. Wylie, Jr. Solve murders and robberies, find out which fishermen are liars, how a blind man could possibly identify a color—purely by your own reasoning! 107pp. 5⅜ × 8½. 20367-0 Pa. $2.50

THE BOOK OF WORLD-FAMOUS MUSIC—CLASSICAL, POPULAR AND FOLK, James J. Fuld. Revised and enlarged republication of landmark work in musico-bibliography. Full information about nearly 1,000 songs and compositions including first lines of music and lyrics. New supplement. Index. 800pp. 5⅜ × 8¼. 24857-7 Pa. $15.95

ANTHROPOLOGY AND MODERN LIFE, Franz Boas. Great anthropologist's classic treatise on race and culture. Introduction by Ruth Bunzel. Only inexpensive paperback edition. 255pp. 5⅜ × 8½. 25245-0 Pa. $6.95

THE TALE OF PETER RABBIT, Beatrix Potter. The inimitable Peter's terrifying adventure in Mr. McGregor's garden, with all 27 wonderful, full-color Potter illustrations. 55pp. 4¼ × 5½. (Available in U.S. only) 22827-4 Pa. $1.75

THREE PROPHETIC SCIENCE FICTION NOVELS, H. G. Wells. *When the Sleeper Wakes, A Story of the Days to Come* and *The Time Machine* (full version). 335pp. 5⅜ × 8½. (Available in U.S. only) 20605-X Pa. $6.95

APICIUS COOKERY AND DINING IN IMPERIAL ROME, edited and translated by Joseph Dommers Vehling. Oldest known cookbook in existence offers readers a clear picture of what foods Romans ate, how they prepared them, etc. 49 illustrations. 301pp. 6⅛ × 9¼. 23563-7 Pa. $7.95

SHAKESPEARE LEXICON AND QUOTATION DICTIONARY, Alexander Schmidt. Full definitions, locations, shades of meaning of every word in plays and poems. More than 50,000 exact quotations. 1,485pp. 6½ × 9¼. 22726-X, 22727-8 Pa., Two-vol. set $29.90

THE WORLD'S GREAT SPEECHES, edited by Lewis Copeland and Lawrence W. Lamm. Vast collection of 278 speeches from Greeks to 1970. Powerful and effective models; unique look at history. 842pp. 5⅜ × 8½. 20468-5 Pa. $11.95

PLANTS OF THE BIBLE, Harold N. Moldenke and Alma L. Moldenke. Standard reference to all 230 plants mentioned in Scriptures. Latin name, biblical reference, uses, modern identity, much more. Unsurpassed encyclopedic resource for scholars, botanists, nature lovers, students of Bible. Bibliography. Indexes. 123 black-and-white illustrations. 384pp. 6 × 9. 25069-5 Pa. $8.95

FAMOUS AMERICAN WOMEN: A Biographical Dictionary from Colonial Times to the Present, Robert McHenry, ed. From Pocahontas to Rosa Parks, 1,035 distinguished American women documented in separate biographical entries. Accurate, up-to-date data, numerous categories, spans 400 years. Indices. 493pp. 6½ × 9¼. 24523-3 Pa. $10.95

THE FABULOUS INTERIORS OF THE GREAT OCEAN LINERS IN HISTORIC PHOTOGRAPHS, William H. Miller, Jr. Some 200 superb photographs capture exquisite interiors of world's great "floating palaces"—1890's to 1980's: *Titanic, Ile de France, Queen Elizabeth, United States, Europa,* more. Approx. 200 black-and-white photographs. Captions. Text. Introduction. 160pp. 8⅞ × 11¾. 24756-2 Pa. $9.95

THE GREAT LUXURY LINERS, 1927-1954: A Photographic Record, William H. Miller, Jr. Nostalgic tribute to heyday of ocean liners. 186 photos of Ile de France, Normandie, Leviathan, Queen Elizabeth, United States, many others. Interior and exterior views. Introduction. Captions. 160pp. 9 × 12. 24056-8 Pa. $10.95

A NATURAL HISTORY OF THE DUCKS, John Charles Phillips. Great landmark of ornithology offers complete detailed coverage of nearly 200 species and subspecies of ducks: gadwall, sheldrake, merganser, pintail, many more. 74 full-color plates, 102 black-and-white. Bibliography. Total of 1,920pp. 8⅝ × 11¼. 25141-1, 25142-X Cloth. Two-vol. set $100.00

THE SEAWEED HANDBOOK: An Illustrated Guide to Seaweeds from North Carolina to Canada, Thomas F. Lee. Concise reference covers 78 species. Scientific and common names, habitat, distribution, more. Finding keys for easy identification. 224pp. 5⅜ × 8½. 25215-9 Pa. $6.95

THE TEN BOOKS OF ARCHITECTURE: The 1755 Leoni Edition, Leon Battista Alberti. Rare classic helped introduce the glories of ancient architecture to the Renaissance. 68 black-and-white plates. 336pp. 8⅜ × 11¼. 25239-6 Pa. $14.95

MISS MACKENZIE, Anthony Trollope. Minor masterpieces by Victorian master unmasks many truths about life in 19th-century England. First inexpensive edition in years. 392pp. 5⅜ × 8½. 25201-9 Pa. $8.95

THE RIME OF THE ANCIENT MARINER, Gustave Doré, Samuel Taylor Coleridge. Dramatic engravings considered by many to be his greatest work. The terrifying space of the open sea, the storms and whirlpools of an unknown ocean, the ice of Antarctica, more—all rendered in a powerful, chilling manner. Full text. 38 plates. 77pp. 9¼ × 12. 22305-1 Pa. $4.95

THE EXPEDITIONS OF ZEBULON MONTGOMERY PIKE, Zebulon Montgomery Pike. Fascinating first-hand accounts (1805-6) of exploration of Mississippi River, Indian wars, capture by Spanish dragoons, much more. 1,088pp. 5⅜ × 8½. 25254-X, 25255-8 Pa. Two-vol. set $25.90

DEGAS: An Intimate Portrait, Ambroise Vollard. Charming, anecdotal memoir by famous art dealer of one of the greatest 19th-century French painters. 14 black-and-white illustrations. Introduction by Harold L. Van Doren. 96pp. 5⅜ × 8½.
25131-4 Pa. $4.95

PERSONAL NARRATIVE OF A PILGRIMAGE TO ALMANDINAH AND MECCAH, Richard Burton. Great travel classic by remarkably colorful personality. Burton, disguised as a Moroccan, visited sacred shrines of Islam, narrowly escaping death. 47 illustrations. 959pp. 5⅜ × 8½. 21217-3, 21218-1 Pa., Two-vol. set $19.90

PHRASE AND WORD ORIGINS, A. H. Holt. Entertaining, reliable, modern study of more than 1,200 colorful words, phrases, origins and histories. Much unexpected information. 254pp. 5⅜ × 8½. 20758-7 Pa. $5.95

THE RED THUMB MARK, R. Austin Freeman. In this first Dr. Thorndyke case, the great scientific detective draws fascinating conclusions from the nature of a single fingerprint. Exciting story, authentic science. 320pp. 5⅜ × 8½. (Available in U.S. only) 25210-8 Pa. $6.95

AN EGYPTIAN HIEROGLYPHIC DICTIONARY, E. A. Wallis Budge. Monumental work containing about 25,000 words or terms that occur in texts ranging from 3000 B.C. to 600 A.D. Each entry consists of a transliteration of the word, the word in hieroglyphs, and the meaning in English. 1,314pp. 6⅞ × 10.
23615-3, 23616-1 Pa., Two-vol. set $31.90

THE COMPLEAT STRATEGYST: Being a Primer on the Theory of Games of Strategy, J. D. Williams. Highly entertaining classic describes, with many illustrated examples, how to select best strategies in conflict situations. Prefaces. Appendices. xvi + 268pp. 5⅜ × 8½. 25101-2 Pa. $5.95

THE ROAD TO OZ, L. Frank Baum. Dorothy meets the Shaggy Man, little Button-Bright and the Rainbow's beautiful daughter in this delightful trip to the magical Land of Oz. 272pp. 5⅜ × 8. 25208-6 Pa. $5.95

POINT AND LINE TO PLANE, Wassily Kandinsky. Seminal exposition of role of point, line, other elements in non-objective painting. Essential to understanding 20th-century art. 127 illustrations. 192pp. 6½ × 9¼. 23808-3 Pa. $4.95

LADY ANNA, Anthony Trollope. Moving chronicle of Countess Lovel's bitter struggle to win for herself and daughter Anna their rightful rank and fortune—perhaps at cost of sanity itself. 384pp. 5⅜ × 8½. 24669-8 Pa. $8.95

EGYPTIAN MAGIC, E. A. Wallis Budge. Sums up all that is known about magic in Ancient Egypt: the role of magic in controlling the gods, powerful amulets that warded off evil spirits, scarabs of immortality, use of wax images, formulas and spells, the secret name, much more. 253pp. 5⅜ × 8½. 22681-6 Pa. $4.50

THE DANCE OF SIVA, Ananda Coomaraswamy. Preeminent authority unfolds the vast metaphysic of India: the revelation of her art, conception of the universe, social organization, etc. 27 reproductions of art masterpieces. 192pp. 5⅜ × 8½.
24817-8 Pa. $5.95

CHRISTMAS CUSTOMS AND TRADITIONS, Clement A. Miles. Origin, evolution, significance of religious, secular practices. Caroling, gifts, yule logs, much more. Full, scholarly yet fascinating; non-sectarian. 400pp. 5⅜ × 8½.
23354-5 Pa. $6.95

THE HUMAN FIGURE IN MOTION, Eadweard Muybridge. More than 4,500 stopped-action photos, in action series, showing undraped men, women, children jumping, lying down, throwing, sitting, wrestling, carrying, etc. 390pp. 7⅞ × 10⅝.
20204-6 Cloth. $21.95

THE MAN WHO WAS THURSDAY, Gilbert Keith Chesterton. Witty, fast-paced novel about a club of anarchists in turn-of-the-century London. Brilliant social, religious, philosophical speculations. 128pp. 5⅜ × 8½. 25121-7 Pa. $3.95

A CEZANNE SKETCHBOOK: Figures, Portraits, Landscapes and Still Lifes, Paul Cezanne. Great artist experiments with tonal effects, light, mass, other qualities in over 100 drawings. A revealing view of developing master painter, precursor of Cubism. 102 black-and-white illustrations. 144pp. 8¾ × 6⅜. 24790-2 Pa. $5.95

AN ENCYCLOPEDIA OF BATTLES: Accounts of Over 1,560 Battles from 1479 B.C. to the Present, David Eggenberger. Presents essential details of every major battle in recorded history, from the first battle of Megiddo in 1479 B.C. to Grenada in 1984. List of Battle Maps. New Appendix covering the years 1967–1984. Index. 99 illustrations. 544pp. 6½ × 9¼. 24913-1 Pa. $14.95

AN ETYMOLOGICAL DICTIONARY OF MODERN ENGLISH, Ernest Weekley. Richest, fullest work, by foremost British lexicographer. Detailed word histories. Inexhaustible. Total of 856pp. 6½ × 9¼.
21873-2, 21874-0 Pa., Two-vol. set $17.00

WEBSTER'S AMERICAN MILITARY BIOGRAPHIES, edited by Robert McHenry. Over 1,000 figures who shaped 3 centuries of American military history. Detailed biographies of Nathan Hale, Douglas MacArthur, Mary Hallaren, others. Chronologies of engagements, more. Introduction. Addenda. 1,033 entries in alphabetical order. xi + 548pp. 6½ × 9¼. (Available in U.S. only)
24758-9 Pa. $13.95

LIFE IN ANCIENT EGYPT, Adolf Erman. Detailed older account, with much not in more recent books: domestic life, religion, magic, medicine, commerce, and whatever else needed for complete picture. Many illustrations. 597pp. 5⅜ × 8½.
22632-8 Pa. $8.95

HISTORIC COSTUME IN PICTURES, Braun & Schneider. Over 1,450 costumed figures shown, covering a wide variety of peoples: kings, emperors, nobles, priests, servants, soldiers, scholars, townsfolk, peasants, merchants, courtiers, cavaliers, and more. 256pp. 8⅜ × 11¼. 23150-X Pa. $9.95

THE NOTEBOOKS OF LEONARDO DA VINCI, edited by J. P. Richter. Extracts from manuscripts reveal great genius; on painting, sculpture, anatomy, sciences, geography, etc. Both Italian and English. 186 ms. pages reproduced, plus 500 additional drawings, including studies for *Last Supper, Sforza* monument, etc. 860pp. 7⅞ × 10¾. (Available in U.S. only) 22572-0, 22573-9 Pa., Two-vol. set $31.90

THE ART NOUVEAU STYLE BOOK OF ALPHONSE MUCHA: All 72 Plates from "Documents Decoratifs" in Original Color, Alphonse Mucha. Rare copyright-free design portfolio by high priest of Art Nouveau. Jewelry, wallpaper, stained glass, furniture, figure studies, plant and animal motifs, etc. Only complete one-volume edition. 80pp. 9⅝ × 12¼. 24044-4 Pa. $9.95

ANIMALS: 1,419 COPYRIGHT-FREE ILLUSTRATIONS OF MAMMALS, BIRDS, FISH, INSECTS, ETC., edited by Jim Harter. Clear wood engravings present, in extremely lifelike poses, over 1,000 species of animals. One of the most extensive pictorial sourcebooks of its kind. Captions. Index. 284pp. 9 × 12. 23766-4 Pa. $9.95

OBELISTS FLY HIGH, C. Daly King. Masterpiece of American detective fiction, long out of print, involves murder on a 1935 transcontinental flight—"a very thrilling story"—NY Times. Unabridged and unaltered republication of the edition published by William Collins Sons & Co. Ltd., London, 1935. 288pp. 5⅜ × 8½. (Available in U.S. only) 25036-9 Pa. $5.95

VICTORIAN AND EDWARDIAN FASHION: A Photographic Survey, Alison Gernsheim. First fashion history completely illustrated by contemporary photographs. Full text plus 235 photos, 1840-1914, in which many celebrities appear. 240pp. 6½ × 9¼. 24205-6 Pa. $6.95

THE ART OF THE FRENCH ILLUSTRATED BOOK, 1700-1914, Gordon N. Ray. Over 630 superb book illustrations by Fragonard, Delacroix, Daumier, Doré, Grandville, Manet, Mucha, Steinlen, Toulouse-Lautrec and many others. Preface. Introduction. 633 halftones. Indices of artists, authors & titles, binders and provenances. Appendices. Bibliography. 608pp. 8⅜ × 11¼. 25086-5 Pa. $24.95

THE WONDERFUL WIZARD OF OZ, L. Frank Baum. Facsimile in full color of America's finest children's classic. 143 illustrations by W. W. Denslow. 267pp. 5⅜ × 8½. 20691-2 Pa. $7.95

FRONTIERS OF MODERN PHYSICS: New Perspectives on Cosmology, Relativity, Black Holes and Extraterrestrial Intelligence, Tony Rothman, et al. For the intelligent layman. Subjects include: cosmological models of the universe; black holes; the neutrino; the search for extraterrestrial intelligence. Introduction. 46 black-and-white illustrations. 192pp. 5⅜ × 8½. 24587-X Pa. $7.95

THE FRIENDLY STARS, Martha Evans Martin & Donald Howard Menzel. Classic text marshalls the stars together in an engaging, non-technical survey, presenting them as sources of beauty in night sky. 23 illustrations. Foreword. 2 star charts. Index. 147pp. 5⅜ × 8½. 21099-5 Pa. $3.95

FADS AND FALLACIES IN THE NAME OF SCIENCE, Martin Gardner. Fair, witty appraisal of cranks, quacks, and quackeries of science and pseudoscience: hollow earth, Velikovsky, orgone energy, Dianetics, flying saucers, Bridey Murphy, food and medical fads, etc. Revised, expanded In the Name of Science. "A very able and even-tempered presentation."—The New Yorker. 363pp. 5⅜ × 8. 20394-8 Pa. $6.95

ANCIENT EGYPT: ITS CULTURE AND HISTORY, J. E Manchip White. From pre-dynastics through Ptolemies: society, history, political structure, religion, daily life, literature, cultural heritage. 48 plates. 217pp. 5⅜ × 8½. 22548-8 Pa. $5.95

SIR HARRY HOTSPUR OF HUMBLETHWAITE, Anthony Trollope. Incisive, unconventional psychological study of a conflict between a wealthy baronet, his idealistic daughter, and their scapegrace cousin. The 1870 novel in its first inexpensive edition in years. 250pp. 5⅜ × 8½. 24953-0 Pa. $5.95

LASERS AND HOLOGRAPHY, Winston E. Kock. Sound introduction to burgeoning field, expanded (1981) for second edition. Wave patterns, coherence, lasers, diffraction, zone plates, properties of holograms, recent advances. 84 illustrations. 160pp. 5⅜ × 8¼. (Except in United Kingdom) 24041-X Pa. $3.95

INTRODUCTION TO ARTIFICIAL INTELLIGENCE: SECOND, ENLARGED EDITION, Philip C. Jackson, Jr. Comprehensive survey of artificial intelligence—the study of how machines (computers) can be made to act intelligently. Includes introductory and advanced material. Extensive notes updating the main text. 132 black-and-white illustrations. 512pp. 5⅜ × 8½. 24864-X Pa. $8.95

HISTORY OF INDIAN AND INDONESIAN ART, Ananda K. Coomaraswamy. Over 400 illustrations illuminate classic study of Indian art from earliest Harappa finds to early 20th century. Provides philosophical, religious and social insights. 304pp. 6⅝ × 9⅝. 25005-9 Pa. $9.95

THE GOLEM, Gustav Meyrink. Most famous supernatural novel in modern European literature, set in Ghetto of Old Prague around 1890. Compelling story of mystical experiences, strange transformations, profound terror. 13 black-and-white illustrations. 224pp. 5⅜ × 8½. (Available in U.S. only) 25025-3 Pa. $6.95

ARMADALE, Wilkie Collins. Third great mystery novel by the author of *The Woman in White* and *The Moonstone*. Original magazine version with 40 illustrations. 597pp. 5⅜ × 8½. 23429-0 Pa. $9.95

PICTORIAL ENCYCLOPEDIA OF HISTORIC ARCHITECTURAL PLANS, DETAILS AND ELEMENTS: With 1,880 Line Drawings of Arches, Domes, Doorways, Facades, Gables, Windows, etc., John Theodore Haneman. Sourcebook of inspiration for architects, designers, others. Bibliography. Captions. 141pp. 9 × 12. 24605-1 Pa. $7.95

BENCHLEY LOST AND FOUND, Robert Benchley. Finest humor from early 30's, about pet peeves, child psychologists, post office and others. Mostly unavailable elsewhere. 73 illustrations by Peter Arno and others. 183pp. 5⅜ × 8½. 22410-4 Pa. $4.95

ERTÉ GRAPHICS, Erté. Collection of striking color graphics: *Seasons, Alphabet, Numerals, Aces* and *Precious Stones*. 50 plates, including 4 on covers. 48pp. 9⅜ × 12¼. 23580-7 Pa. $6.95

THE JOURNAL OF HENRY D. THOREAU, edited by Bradford Torrey, F. H. Allen. Complete reprinting of 14 volumes, 1837-61, over two million words; the sourcebooks for *Walden*, etc. Definitive. All original sketches, plus 75 photographs. 1,804pp. 8½ × 12¼. 20312-3, 20313-1 Cloth., Two-vol. set $120.00

CASTLES: THEIR CONSTRUCTION AND HISTORY, Sidney Toy. Traces castle development from ancient roots. Nearly 200 photographs and drawings illustrate moats, keeps, baileys, many other features. Caernarvon, Dover Castles, Hadrian's Wall, Tower of London, dozens more. 256pp. 5⅜ × 8¼. 24898-4 Pa. $6.95